HIS LORDSHIP'S CHAPERONE

●

Shirley Marks

AVALON BOOKS
NEW YORK

Published by Thomas Bouregy & Co., Inc.
160 Madison Avenue, New York, NY 10016

Library of Congress Cataloging-in-Publication Data

Marks, Shirley.
His lordship's chaperone / Shirley Marks.
p.   cm.
ISBN 978-0-8034-9947-8 (hardcover : acid-free paper)
1. Aristocracy (Social class)—England—Fiction.   I. Title.

PS3613.A7655H57   2009
813'.6—dc22

2008048219

PRINTED IN THE UNITED STATES OF AMERICA
ON ACID-FREE PAPER
BY HADDON CRAFTSMEN, BLOOMSBURG, PENNSYLVANIA

Chapter One

Robert Moreland, the Marquess of Haverton, stood in Lord Brayburn's library for what he thought was a moment of solitude. He was not alone. Lady Joanna had been hiding in the darkened corner, working up the courage to finally speak.

"Is there something in particular I can help you look for, my lord?" It took her another few minutes until she mustered the nerve to touch him. She ran her hand up his sleeve before acquiring the ultimate audacity to slide into his arms. "My father owns some fine leather–bound Shakespeare volumes and many ancient history studies if that is where your interests lie."

"I'm finding much more than I ever expected."

Lady Joanna was not referring to reading material;

1

neither was he. What else could he say? Anything more would have been presumptuous. Anything less an insult.

Haverton smiled. He knew exactly why she was here. It was not that he found her at all unpleasant. Lady Joanna was quite lovely and the Marquess could well appreciate her charms. However there would be no time for that. By the sound of the approaching footsteps, reinforcements were on their way. He and Lady Joanna would not be alone for much longer.

"Thank you for your kind invitation but I fear I must decline." He stepped away from her and moved toward the window, leaving Lady Joanna to stare expectantly at the door. Haverton gripped the window frame and pulled himself outside onto the ledge.

"Ah ha!" cried Lady Brayburn, bursting into the room with Lady Joanna's discarded chaperone trailing.

"I told you Lady Joanna should not have been left alone, my lady!" the chaperone scolded. "What if some gentleman had trapped her behind closed doors and had his evil way with her?"

If Haverton had not been mistaken, that is precisely what Lady Brayburn had been hoping. Lady Joanna had done her best to tempt him but her stilted behavior told him she was a mere innocent following instructions—most likely her mother's.

"Well . . . where is he?" Lady Brayburn sounded most anxious and very cross.

"He's gone, Mama." Lady Joanna's failure was apparent in her voice. "Lord Haverton could not have gone far. He was here just a moment ago."

The thumping and shuffling from inside told the Marquess the ladies were busy searching the room, looking around the furniture and behind the window draperies.

"Did you make yourself available to him?" asked Lady Brayburn.

"Yes, Mama, I did. I allowed him to–to—I did just as you told me."

"How could he have refused your invitation?"

"I do not know, Mama."

"Did you approach him as I showed you?"

It was astounding what a mother would have her daughter do to snag a husband. This had been by far the most outrageous.

"Yes, Mama, I did. He seemed to be taken with me for the moment"—Lady Joanna sounded on the verge of tears—"and I tried to—just as you instructed me, Mama."

"What is wrong with the man? You gave him every opportunity to—"

"My lady!" the chaperone squeaked.

Lady Joanna's sobbing overrode her answer.

Too bad Lady Brayburn had missed her daughter's performance—it had been quite a spectacle. Haverton chuckled, momentarily forgetting the necessity that he remain quiet. After all, he was hiding.

As amusing as it was to listen to the disappointed

women, Haverton had to get back to the gathering belowstairs. Lady Brayburn might get the idea to look out the window. Then where would he be?

He shuffled across the ledge to the room next door. Jumping in, he landed quite neatly on the edge of the Persian carpet. Haverton took a few moments to compose himself. He smoothed back his hair, adjusted his cravat and straightened his coat. Checking to make sure the hallway was clear before stepping out of his hiding place, the Marquess headed for the main drawing room.

It seemed his popularity grew as time passed. Year by year the number of bachelors in Town grew smaller. Marriage was a fate they all faced, he supposed. However this business of trapping him for marriage was becoming very tiresome indeed.

This had been the worst year yet and the Season had two weeks before it officially started. This year, he swore to himself, steps needed to be taken to prevent another such incident from occurring. He needed to do something to keep from always having to hide from or avoid the fortune-hunting ladies, matchmaking mamas, and assorted forward females.

For all the pleasure a gentleman could derive from women, ladies made his life a living hell. Without question, something would have to be done.

In one of the corners of the main drawing room, Lady Stratton chuckled and proceeded with her story. "After all the guests had left, it seems Lord Haverton dressed up as one of the footmen and slipped back into the house. Lady Firth had already gone to bed. As I hear it, Lord Firth was busy working late in his study."

"Had they arranged it all at the party?" Lady Clare inquired from behind her open fan.

"I cannot be sure," Lady Stratton continued. "Although I hear tell there had been some shameless flirting between them during dinner."

"I've heard that he's broken off with Mrs. Cummings-Albright," Mrs. Baldwin added. "It happened last year at the end of the Season."

"No wonder he's so bold. Lack of female companionship will do that to a man," Lady Clare replied knowingly.

Lady Stratton and Mrs. Baldwin froze and stared at Lady Clare.

"And how would you know?" Mrs. Baldwin asked. "Have you, by chance, had a rendezvous with him?"

Lady Clare blushed. "Of course not! But don't we all wish we could?" She giggled like an empty-headed schoolgirl. The other two ladies didn't behave much better. They chuckled too.

Stuff and nonsense. The Duchess of Waverly wished she had stepped away from the trio the first time she heard her son's name mentioned. Why had she insisted on listening to the gossip? Gossip was just that—gossip. No real facts were involved, she reminded herself. Except she knew there was always some shred of truth in any rumor.

The Duchess knew Robert had wintered in Sussex. A few months before, he had courted Mrs. Cummings-Albright and a few months later they parted company. In the Lady Firth fiction, the one piece of truth might have been that Robert had attended a dinner party at the Firth Lodge without Mrs. Cummings-Albright.

The rest of the overblown tale—sneaking into the house after hours—could be just pure speculation or some bit of wishful thinking on the part of Lady Firth. Anyone, any *female* that is, would delight in any type of an association with the Duchess' rich, charming, and handsome son.

Which brought Her to lament that Robert was much too rich, extremely too charming, and far too handsome for his own good. Although he had managed to handle the combination well, he tended to take most things for granted. That was his problem. He could do whatever he liked with whomever he wished.

Yes, she mused, things came much too easy for him. What his life needed was stability and direction. He had only a few more years before he reached the age of thirty. It was certainly time he provided an heir. Each and every Season that passed she had insisted he find a bride but this was the year the Duchess expected results.

It *was* high time Robert married.

Haverton stood in the doorway of the main drawing room and observed the members of the *ton*. Couples danced and, off to the side, others held private conversations. Across the room in another corner sat the dowagers, companions, and abandoned chaperones. Chaperones whose charges had escaped their attention, no doubt.

How many poor fools would fall prey to some female's set of contrived circumstances? Not all men were as well practiced as he at avoiding the modern day female. Keeping company with a married woman or a young widow was far preferable to any milk and water miss.

He understood society's rules concerning safeguarding innocent girls, but their chaperones were discarded at a time when, he believed, they were most needed. It seemed to him that chaperones were more useful protecting a gentleman's freedom. Haverton stilled when the idea struck him.

Chaperones.

But of course, why hadn't he thought of this before?

If the women of London insisted on leaving their chaperones behind, he saw no alternative but to supply one of his own. Make no mistake, it would not be for the ladies but for his own protection.

A brilliant, if not novel, notion and an entirely sound course of action. Nothing he could do about it presently. He could proceed first thing tomorrow—that was, if he could survive tonight.

"There you are, Robert."

Haverton nearly jumped out of his skin when his brother called out to him.

"I'm sorry." Simon clapped Haverton on the shoulder. "I didn't expect to scare you."

"I thought you might be someone else."

"Who were you expecting?"

"Lord Brayburn," Haverton confessed with a whisper.

"Good Gad, why?"

Haverton ran his hand down his waistcoat, smoothing any imperfections he might have missed. "His daughter, Lady Joanna, managed to corner me in his library."

Simon's eyes widened. "I thought you knew better than to wander off by yourself."

"I needed to get away for just a bit." Haverton squeezed his eyes closed and pinched the bridge of his nose, preparing himself for the torment that was sure to follow. "I thought I had seen enough of tonight's festivities. Apparently I hadn't seen enough. While in the library, Lady Joanna arrived and did her best to find a diversion to the merriment of the ballroom."

Simon laughed.

"And while I freely admit that she is a diamond of the first water, Lord Brayburn's library does not inspire me as the proper place for cultivating romance." Experience told Haverton that nothing would halt his brother's outburst. He had to stand there and tolerate it or make a scene fleeing. His early departure would certainly cause nothing short of a scandal.

"She's quite a fetching thing. I think you would have dug your heels in and enjoyed yourself."

"On the contrary, I escaped and managed to keep my

virtue intact." Haverton's reply brought a fresh bout of laughter from his brother. "Had I not been on the alert, I would have been caught in that neat web designed by Lady Brayburn."

"Good thing you're fleet of foot."

"Yes, but the years are catching up." He sighed and tried to sound as tired and aged as possible. "I'm not as young as I used to be."

"You managed to escape quite unharmed," Simon said, sounding wholly unsympathetic.

"For the moment but I did sustain a superficial injury." Haverton felt for the small torn seam under his arm. "Another incident such as that and I'll be reduced to my shirtsleeves. What is it about desperate women?"

"As I understand it, this will be her second Season. I'm of the opinion that Lady Brayburn expects her daughter to marry this year. If she's after you, then she wishes her daughter to marry well."

Haverton glanced around the room, checking to see if Lady Brayburn and Lady Joanna had returned. "Fine. All the best to her I say. I'll be more than glad to wish the couple happy and to attend their ceremony. But she'll not wed me."

"How do you do it, Robert? How do you fight off the scores of women who relentlessly hound you at these affairs? Gad, I don't have half the problem you do."

"You exaggerate, Simon. I am not pursued by *scores* of women."

"From what I understand, it's when you single them

out you get into trouble." Simon's laughter diminished to a mild chuckle under Haverton's quelling gaze. "I've heard that you've been busy since I saw you last at father's hunting lodge at the end of last year."

Haverton raised his eyebrow and regarded Simon skeptically. "I dread to ask it but what exactly have you heard?"

"Something about you attending a dinner party and sneaking back into the house for a very early morning rendezvous with the hostess after all the guests had left." Simon shook his finger at his brother. "I thought you knew better than to tryst with the lady of the house. Shows extremely bad form, lack of respect to your host and that sort of thing."

"Simon, I thought you'd know better than to listen to idle gossip. And the facts are very, very wrong." Haverton laughed, but the twisted tale really wasn't funny— just the abstract turn it had taken. "The truth of the matter was I tried to sneak *out*, not in. Lady Firth was the one who locked me in her closet, saving me for dessert." He exhaled in exasperation. "What's the use? I think you would know me well enough. Would I really do such a thing?"

"I thought there might be a rational explanation. I just wanted to see the look on your face when you discovered what's being said about you."

"I imagine that's not the half of it. I am not so desperate for female companionship as to dally with the hostess of the party I'm attending."

"You know how to put an end to it all."

"Stop right there." Haverton held up his hand. "Not another word."

"You know what Mother thinks . . ." Simon shrugged.

"Speaking of Mother, where is she?" Haverton glanced about the room. He was sure he had seen her here earlier. Or was that at last night's soiree?

"Mother?" Simon pivoted, glancing about the room. "I think she's over there." He pointed to a corner. "Do you see her standing with Lady Clare?"

Haverton looked over the crowd. "Ah, yes."

"Why the devil do you want to see Mother? You're usually trying to avoid her."

"I am in need of her social contacts." Exactly how he would explain that he needed a chaperone for himself was another matter.

"It's not to meet a certain lady is it?"

"You are precisely right—it is to meet a woman."

"You know she won't help you set up any questionable associations. Much rather you were seeing to an heir."

"It's not what you think." Haverton smiled. "I need a particular sort of woman." He had until tomorrow to come up with the proper phrasing.

"You're asking for trouble." Simon shook his head. "Don't you think you've had enough of females?"

"I've always maintained that I've had the lion's share—" Haverton stopped abruptly when Miss Emma Dunstead slowed to stroll by at an amazingly slow pace.

He made eye contact and returned her tempting smile. "I have no objection to the ladies' attentions, as it were . . ."

Miss Dunstead had blossomed from a slightly awkward young lady into the fine woman standing before him. Her delightful blue eyes, exquisitely dainty nose, and most perfect rosebud lips added to her newfound beauty. A wisp of dark hair feathered across her forehead and framed her heart-shaped face.

"I do, however, take exception to their impulsive rush to the altar," Haverton concluded.

Simon shifted his attention from his brother to Miss Dunstead. "It's the way you look at them. What a talent! You make them fall in love with you just by looking at them."

"In love with me?" Glancing back again at the young lady, Haverton noted Miss Dunstead still looked his way and never seemed to notice Simon's presence. "Nothing is further from my mind. I cannot prevent them reading something in my eyes that is not there."

She was far too young and far too dangerous for a chance meeting. Miss Dunstead was exactly the type that should be avoided.

"It may not be intentional on your part, but you certainly do pay the consequences for their misinterpretations."

"You may be right but I shall not be paying much longer." Haverton smiled wide and fully satisfied. "I believe I have found the answer to my problems."

* * *

Why do I bother attending these functions? The Duchess of Waverly summed up the evening as fairly uneventful. That was until she spotted her eldest son Robert coming her way.

He edged around the dance floor and skirted around the groups of guests lost in conversation. The ladies, she noticed, were not so involved and with the exception of two or three, glanced at him with longing as he made his way past.

"Good evening to you, ladies . . . Lady Stratton." The Duchess watched Robert gaze into Lady Stratton's eyes, bent over her proffered gloved hand.

"Lord Haverton," Lady Stratton returned. "Charmed, I assure you."

Why does he waste his glorious charm on these old bats? the Duchess silently chided. He was far from needing the practice.

"Lady Clare." Robert took his time to pay her the same attention as he had Lady Stratton.

"Lord Haverton, I am so very delighted."

Of course you are, you twit. The Duchess of Waverly popped open her fan.

"And, of course, Mrs. Baldwin." Robert turned to the last lady, smiled and bent over her hand.

"Your lordship," she said and curtsied.

Encroaching mushroom. The Duchess of Waverly fanned herself vigorously.

Robert straightened and his eyes twinkled, making Mrs. Baldwin's blush deepen.

It was enough to make one ill. The Duchess of Waverly closed her fan with a snap.

"Here now, Haverton, come see your mama." The Duchess waved the closed fan at her son, beckoning him near.

"If you will excuse me, ladies." He bowed to them and retreated.

"Disgusting performance," the Duchess greeted her son.

"But no other woman could hold the place in my heart as you do." He took her hand to do the pretty.

She pulled her hand from him. "Of course not, I am your mother."

"And correct, as usual." A smile sailed across his face.

Something was going on with him. She could feel it. "What is it you want, dear?"

"I would like permission to call tomorrow."

"Naturally. So good of you to ask," she responded, dryly.

"Shall we say"—he thought for a moment—"two?"

"I'm not sure I can wait until then. Come for breakfast. Let's say nine. I'll be expecting you."

"I shall be there." Robert bowed to his mother and left.

The Duchess of Waverly dropped her fan open, waved it slowly, and watched him walk away. *What could he possibly be up to now?*

* * *

After taking the first steps toward finding a chaperone, Haverton stood with his brother. "It's all settled. I'll speak to her tomorrow morning at nine."

"I'll be dashing off to White's to wager that she'll not like your coming to her for a woman." One side of Simon's mouth quirked up into a half smile.

"I believe everything will work out quite satisfactorily." Haverton clapped his brother on the back and headed for the garden.

He stepped outside and took a deep breath of cool night air. Was the air really fresher? Did it smell sweeter? Or was it because his future looked brighter? Haverton had every confidence his mother would know exactly what to do and whom to employ. She always had, from his butler to the upstairs maid.

The sound of the water trickling from the fountain added to the serenity of the setting. The shuffling of feet and a muffled protest, a *female* protest, from the shadows beyond the fountain, interrupted his tranquility.

"Stop it!" a woman's voice called out while struggling. "Let go of me!"

Haverton came around the corner and saw the struggling couple. "Yes," he concurred, and ordered, "Let go of that young woman at once!"

Miss Emma Dunstead ran from the shadows into the sanctuary of Haverton's arms. The over-amorous suitor ran off in the opposite direction. Torn between pursuing the knave and comforting the shaken Miss Dunstead,

Haverton found her warmth and feminine curves difficult to resist and impossible to abandon.

Her wide blue eyes gazed up at him. "Lord Haverton, is it not?"

"We had the pleasure of an introduction last Season,"
he reminded her. Miss Dunstead shivered in his arms.
Clearly she was not over her ordeal.

"A moment, if you please." She pushed him away
and stood alone, bathed in the silvery moonlight next
to the over-sized garden fountain. Haverton admired
the outline of her figure—it could not have been more
perfect.

"I thank you for coming to my aid, sir." Miss Dunstead had a voice of an angel.

"The pleasure is all mine." The soothing sound of the
running water gave him the same serene, tranquil feeling he had experienced earlier, before the commotion
of Miss Dunstead's unpleasant incident.

She moved toward the far side of the fountain, placed
her palm to her forehead, and gave a soft, quiet sigh.

If one stood directly behind the fountain, Haverton
noted, one could be hidden from the view of the on-
lookers in the drawing room. While he knew under nor-
mal circumstances he would not place himself in this
kind of situation, he felt responsible, if only temporar-
ily, for her well-being.

"Are you feeling unwell?" Ignoring his instincts, he
approached her. "Shall I fetch—"

"My lord," she crooned, and reached out her arm to

him. "Haverton?" she said in a sigh. "May I call you Haverton?"

"If you would like." Although he thought it far too familiar.

"Yes, I would like very much." She leaned against him for support in her weakened condition, gazed up at him, once again leaving him to stare into her amazing blue eyes.

"Could it really be true that I paid you no notice last Season?" He studied her remarkable features once again.

"I'm afraid that is so," she admitted. "Not that I had many suitors to turn down—it would have hurt me to say no to you."

Miss Dunstead's lips pursed in the most adorable way when she said no.

"Mama thought I should wait until this Season to marry." She glanced up at him again and smiled. "I'm so glad I did." Miss Dunstead fingered the folds of his cravat. "I had heard some rather curious things about you."

"Wild gossip, no doubt."

"Is none of it true?" She sounded disappointed.

"You cannot believe everything you hear. Some gossip is meant to cause harm, some is to further the wild tale for enjoyment sake, and some is talk from those who are merely jealous."

"And which category would I fall under?"

"You? I should hope you would not kiss and tell."

"But I have not yet been kissed," she announced, almost as a challenge.

"No, not as of yet." Haverton tilted her chin with his finger, she was so cooperative and willing to allow him to do as he wished. He had no doubt that she *was* definitely the kiss-and-tell type.

What on earth was he doing here anyway? If he were caught alone with her . . .

As discreetly as he could manage, the Marquess surveyed the courtyard. It was surrounded by ground floor buildings. One set of French doors led into the ballroom. Opposite the ballroom entrance was a darkened path which, at present, echoed approaching footsteps. Miss Dunstead grabbed hold of his jacket sleeves, preventing his retreat.

"What's the matter?" she cried, as if he hadn't noticed what was about to happen.

It was another trap.

He glanced about him. The fountain was the only structure around. Her head turned in one direction then the other, glancing over each shoulder, looking, waiting for them . . .

He managed to pull free from her grasp but there was no place for the Marquess to hide—only the fountain. The fountain . . . Haverton stepped into the cold, cold water and stifled a gasp. With amazing speed he got down on his hands and knees. He took a large gulp of air, held his breath and laid spread-eagle in the pond.

He could barely hear muffled voices over the cascading water of the fountain. They wondered where he had gone off to, no doubt. Whoever *they* were. Haverton wished they'd go inside to display their amazement at his disappearing act.

Leave! Please leave before I run out of air!

Haverton had no choice. His lungs were about to explode. He had to come up for air.

Lifting his head, he broke the surface of the water trying to draw as little attention to himself as possible. He looked around—no one. He was alone. The Marquess pushed up to a sitting position then stood. He was not pleased with the way things had turned out. Not at all.

His once immaculate and well-crafted cravat was now a drooping wet rag. Water drained from his sleeves and dripped from the hem of his new Weston jacket. His breeches clung to him in the most uncomfortable manner. This set of clothes would never be the same again.

Haverton pulled a long, slimy piece of pond growth from his shoulder and tossed it back into the water. He wrung the tail of his jacket.

The evening, at least for him, was at an end. It was time to go home. He left a trail of water on his way to find his carriage and reassured himself that tomorrow everything would change.

Chapter Two

The Marquess of Haverton arrived at Waverly House precisely ten minutes before the hour of nine. It was necessary to do so in order to listen to one of his mother's rare praises.

"It's precisely nine o'clock and here you are." She opened her napkin and laid it upon her lap.

Haverton returned from the sideboard with his breakfast plate and took the seat next to his mother. "If I remember correctly, Mother, are you not the one who insists on arriving at the table on time or waiting until the next meal?"

"Oh, you do remember your childhood, how sweet." The Duchess nodded to Mary to pour the coffee.

"You were a bit strict on that point—as well as many others, if I recall correctly." In truth the details of his childhood were mainly a blur but he'd never admit such a thing to his parent.

"Discipline is the backbone of authority. *I*"—she announced imperiously—"had to raise a duke."

"Hopefully that is in the distant future. I do not look forward to taking that step." He gestured to Mary to fill his coffee cup.

"And why is that, dear?" The Duchess straightened the edges of the white linen napkin on her lap.

"The added responsibility, I suppose." He brought the cup to his lips and blew onto the coffee. "I wish father a very long and healthy life." For the most part Haverton enjoyed his life. After this morning's discussion he expected his life would take a turn for the better.

"How kind of you." Her Grace stirred cream and sugar in her coffee.

"Which brings me to why I'm here. I am in need of your help." Haverton came straight to the point. *That* he had also learned from his mother.

The Duchess closed her eyes and pressed her palms together in front of her. "My dear, dear boy. You've finally come to your senses, haven't you?"

"I would like to think so." He took a bite of sausage and imagined attending festivities without having to look around the corner for a young lady who lay in wait to compromise him. He could enjoy the party with his friends, amuse himself with mild flirtation with the ladies, and even dance a set or two!

"You're ready to wed and you've come to your

resourceful mother for a list of suitable brides." She gestured in the air with her fork.

"Ah . . . no, that's not quite it." Marriage? He wasn't thinking anything of the sort. "I was hoping to enlist my resourceful mother to help me find a suitable chaperone."

The Duchess exhaled in an exasperated manner, and she replaced her fork on the table—rather loudly. "Of all the—I am most displeased."

Haverton glanced skyward and drew a slow breath.

"Isn't it enough that you are the *Rogue of the Realm*?"

"Mother, I think that may be a bit of an exaggeration—" That was a ridiculous moniker.

"Do not interrupt me," she shot back. "It is not enough that I must put up with the gossip? And let me tell you I've already had an earful since I've returned to Town."

"But Mother . . . the gossip is only—"

"I do not know who you expect to disguise in a blanket of propriety. It will not work, I tell you, and I refuse to be a part of it. You will receive no help from this quarter." She picked up her fork, stabbed her slab of ham and dug into it with a knife.

"Mother, if you'd only listen—please. I am not the grand seducer they may say I am. Quite the contrary—and I do not chase young ladies. This is the exact type of outrage I wish to end." Haverton exhaled. This was all becoming very tiresome. "I plan on taking steps to prevent just this sort of thing from happening."

"Steps? What steps?" She looked up from her plate.

"The chaperone I am inquiring about is for me," he said with perfect calm.

"Do you mean to tell me . . ." The fork and knife in the Duchess' hands fell onto the plate with a clatter.

Haverton left his seat and rushed to her aid.

"The family . . . the disgrace . . ." Her eyes fluttered shut, and she slid from her chair, landing gracefully on the floor.

He carried his mother to the small sofa next to the window. "Mother? Mother?" He patted her hand to help revive her. "Come now, Mother. Wake up."

Mary came from the kitchen. Out of one of the sideboard drawers, she pulled a vinaigrette bottle, uncorked it and waved it under the Duchess' nose.

Her Grace opened her eyes. "Get away!" She waved her arms, forcing Mary back. "What has happened?"

Haverton dismissed the servant girl and helped his mother sit upright. "I was telling you of my desire to employ a chaperone."

The Duchess gasped. "Oh . . . I thought it was all a bad dream." She pressed her fingers to her temples and a pained expression crossed her face.

"Do you not see that it is the answer to all my problems?" Haverton had hoped he could bring her around to his way of thinking.

She lamented, "I had hoped that the madness of your father's Uncle Clarence would pass our family—"

"Mother, I am serious."

She continued to stare at him. "So am I. You shall be the laughingstock of London."

"Then I shall be an unattached laughingstock. You simply do not understand what I endure. I cannot continue being preyed upon any longer. I am more than happy to provide a chaperone for the lady who insists on keeping my company without her escort. It is the least I can do."

"How magnanimous of you." Her Grace stretched out her arm and waited for her son to help her to her feet.

Haverton slid his arm around her waist and helped her gain her balance. "I admit I am not thinking solely of the young lady."

"*That* would be a first—you thinking of someone other than yourself." She once again settled into her chair.

"Would you wish me to become entangled in an association not of my choosing?" He walked to his place but did not sit. Haverton would not stand here and allow his mother to dictate when he should marry or to whom. "You need not aid me in finding someone suitable, if that is what you wish. I can utilize other sources to gain my ends."

The Duchess remained momentarily silent. Haverton wondered if she was listening to him at all.

"If that is what you wish, Mother. I thank you for the breakfast. I'll be on my way now." He headed for the door.

"Just a moment."

Haverton stopped and faced her.

"On second thought, I believe I shall make a few inquiries on your behalf."

"Excellent." The Marquess strode to his mother and kissed her on the cheek. It did not matter what he said to change her mind. All he cared about was she had. "I can't tell you how much this means to me."

"After giving it some thought, perhaps this might work out well for you."

Haverton stepped forward, pleased by his mother's approval. "You can guarantee her excellent living conditions and a generous salary. Her character must be above reproach. I want someone upstanding and completely reliable. I want only the best."

"Yes, dear," the Duchess concurred. "For you, I would only settle for the very best."

The Talbots' butler allowed Miss Catherine Hayward's visitor, the Duchess of Waverly, to enter the mansion through the front door and led her to the front parlor.

"I have instructed Roxanne to watch Master Thomas and Miss Chloe while you attend to your visitor." Hopkins' disapproval was clear.

First of all, Catherine should not have visitors, and Duchess or not, they should not be calling at the front door. However, one did not expect a Duchess to call at the servants' entrance.

"I'm sorry, Mr. Hopkins." Catherine rose out of the

chair and handed baby Chloe to Roxanne. "I had no idea she would ever call on me here."

With an agitated glare, he cleared his throat. "Her Grace is waiting in the front parlor," he said and left.

"Tommy, you be a good lad and mind Roxanne while I'm gone. I'll be back soon." Catherine addressed the young boy stacking blocks on the floor. She glanced down at her dress. There wasn't time to change her clothes without keeping the Duchess waiting. To keep her absence from the nursery as short as possible, Catherine headed to the parlor straight away.

She had met Her Grace only one time, shortly after her arrival in London. There was a polite note from the Duchess once a year, inquiring as to Catherine's health and her satisfaction with her position. The last thing she had expected was a personal call from the lady herself.

On her way down the staircase, Catherine removed her apron, straightened her dress, and smoothed her hair back to her bun. She stopped just outside the parlor doors and slid her reading spectacles low on the bridge of her nose. They always made her look older, more learned, or so she thought anyway.

The Duchess of Waverly stood when Catherine entered the room. "Miss Hayward, how delightful it is to see you again."

Catherine curtsied. "Your Grace."

"I suppose we must stick to protocol in these matters." The Duchess sat and gestured for Catherine to sit beside her.

"Would you care for tea?" Catherine inquired after settling onto the sofa.

"No, thank you. I believe I will get straight to the point of my visit."

That would be nice.

The Duchess leaned the slightest bit forward. "I have a new, and I believe very advantageous, position to offer you."

"But I have been very happy here, Your Grace." Catherine loved her position and she had grown very fond of the four children in her care.

"Lord and Lady Talbot are very pleased with you. But I must tell you this new position will result in double your present wages."

"Double?" Catherine had no doubt her eyes had widened and could only hope her jaw had not dropped open. "I can hardly believe—it's very generous."

"Just as I told you. It is one, I should say, that would be very difficult to decline."

Catherine felt breathless. "What . . . what is this position?"

"Chaperone."

"Chaperone? A lady's chaperone?" Catherine allowed herself to imagine the circumstance for a moment. What a nice change that would be. Gowns and parties instead of nappies and tantrums.

"Not precisely." The Duchess chuckled. "You would be chaperone to my eldest son the Marquess of Haverton."

Catherine clapped her hand over her mouth but not in

time to stop a burst of laugher. "I'm sorry, Your Grace. A chaperone for a man?"

"I know it sounds peculiar but when you meet him I'm sure you will understand. Haverton is a most extraordinary man."

"I don't know." Catherine felt very reluctant to leave her employers and the Talbot children. Except for the money, why should she ever consider leaving?

"You shall have run of the house," Her Grace continued while Catherine remained silent. "You need only accompany the Marquess in the evenings when he attends social gatherings. He really has no need of you during the day—unless, on the off chance, he should attend an afternoon fete or boating party."

She watched Catherine for a reaction. "You should have most of your days to yourself. You must admit," she continued, "watching a grown man for an evening and an occasional afternoon is much better than a house full of children all day long."

The Duchess knew exactly how to get her point across.

"You make the offer sound most attractive."

"I need not make it sound attractive, it is an excellent opportunity. I should think it is one you cannot refuse."

Her Grace was right. Catherine thought of the money she sent to her mother and her three younger sisters. With an increase she would be able to send much, much more. "How can I say no?"

"How very wonderful." The Duchess stood.

"I would like to wait until Lady Talbot can find a replacement for me."

"You may rest assured I have someone in mind to fill your position." Her Grace straightened the strings of her reticule. "Now that you will be installed at Moreland Manor, we shall have tea together as often as we wish."

Catherine walked the Duchess to the front door. "Thank you very much, Your Grace." She dipped into a curtsy. "You are so very kind to care for my family."

"If your mother would only let me do more. But she is a proud woman."

Catherine knew her mother would never take charity from anyone. She depended on the hard work of her four daughters and the occasional kindness from others. For some reason unknown to Catherine, the Duchess of Waverly had always proved to be very kind.

The Duchess placed her gloved hand upon Catherine's. "I shall come by on Sunday at two o'clock and see you to Moreland Manor myself."

Astonished by Her Grace's visit, Catherine could hardly believe that by the end of next week she would meet her new employer. She did not hazard a guess at what would come next in her life or what new and amazing things might happen to her as the chaperone to the Marquess of Haverton.

An hour later, the Waverly-crested coach came to a stop in front of Moreland Manor. The Duchess found her eldest son at home. Rarely did he go anywhere during the day but that might all change with the arrival of Miss Hayward. He seemed to believe that she was the answer to all of his problems.

Robert met his mother as she entered through the front doors and escorted her to the drawing room, and finally led her to her favorite chair. "You're just in time for tea."

"Excellent." The Duchess worked at pulling off her gloves and glanced at the tea tray sitting on the low table before her.

"You have news of my chaperone, do you not?" He settled on the sofa and sat forward, showing his interest. "Tell me all about her."

That would be the day, when she tells him all.

"I shall accompany her here on Sunday," she said simply.

"Sunday, you say?" Then his attention began to wane and he stared out the large picture window.

"Yes, dear, Sunday." The Duchess had expected him to show a little more enthusiasm. After all, this had been his idea.

"Good. I'll have the staff expect her then."

The Duchess could not imagine what was more interesting on the other side of the window than what she was saying in this room. After all, her news was about the chaperone he had been so insistent she hire for him. "I had mentioned to her that she would have run of the house." She laid her gloves on her lap and took up the pot to pour.

"What do you mean 'run of the house?' " He blinked and turned away from the window to stare at her.

"Dear, what do you expect her to do all day long? Stay in her rooms?" Her Grace set the pot down and took up her tea. "She has no other duties except to tend you."

"Rooms?" Robert retrieved his tea, holding the cup to his lips, before taking a sip. "Wait a minute—who said anything about her living in *rooms*?"

"I thought she might stay in the gold suite. Oh, look at these delicious biscuits . . . fresh, aren't they?" The Duchess sampled one of the freshly baked treats. They tasted as good as they smelled.

"The gold suite? But that is the largest of the guest quarters." Robert set his cup and saucer down, without consideration of the delicate bone china. "It seems most inappropriate."

"She must be comfortable, and you can't expect her to come pelting down three flights of stairs at the snap of your fingers." The Duchess snapped her fingers, displaying what her son ought not to do. "She is to be at your beck and call, is she not? Can't expect her to sleep in the attic."

"I suppose not." Robert lifted the tea cup off the saucer and sounded a bit baffled. "All right, she can stay in the gold suite."

"And I've informed her that you would give her a twenty pound advance—which is completely separate from her wages." The Duchess had said no such thing to Miss Hayward that afternoon. She merely wished to see if she could cause him to react, he was quite good at wearing his mask of indifference.

He pulled the rim of the cup away, never taking a sip. "An advance? Is it customary?"

"I should think you would wish her to have accessories for her new gowns."

"Gowns? What new gowns?" His cup hit the saucer.

"I think you might agree that she needs something more appropriate than brown serge. That is if you intend her to accompany you out at night without drawing attention. After all, her previous post was as a governess."

Robert gave an exasperated sigh and mumbled, "She is sounding more trouble than a wife."

Which had not gone unheard by his mother. "What's that you say?"

"I said she sounds as if she has terrible life. You're absolutely right, Mother. I can't possibly have that."

"You are her employer and her appearance does reflect upon you, does it not?"

"Of course it does."

"Then you should supply her with suitable attire, I should think." The Duchess sipped her tea, replaced the china cup on its saucer, and set it on the low table.

"I do not feel that would be completely out of the question." Robert sounded most resigned. "Next you'll be telling me she'll require a lady's maid."

"What an excellent idea!" Her Grace thought that an

inspired suggestion. She realized it was made in jest but it was well done of him.

"Absolutely not!"

"Of course the maid would be in addition to her sixty-four pounds a year." She ignored his protest.

"Sixty-four pounds? That must be at least twice—if not three times her current wage."

"I can see the mathematics tutor we hired in your youth did a fine job with you, dear."

"You promised her sixty-four pounds a year?"

"I promised *you'd* pay her sixty-four pounds a year." The Duchess tugged on a glove. "She needed an incentive to take this . . . unusual position. You must make concessions."

"But Mother, really—" Robert's eyes widened.

"I would have thought the price of your freedom was worth at least that." She stood to leave.

"I had not considered that." He fell silent as if he took a moment to digest their entire conversation. "I suppose you are right."

"Don't be a simpleton, of course I am." The Duchess paused and faced him one last time. "Oh, by the by, do you wish to know her name?"

"Ah, yes, I suppose I must sooner or later." He stood to see his mother to the door.

"Her name is Miss Catherine Hayward."

Robert's lips moved. The Duchess wondered if it was truly sinking in.

"Very well, then. I shall expect her on . . ." Robert turned to his mother. "What day did you say she was to arrive? Next Monday?"

"Sunday!" It was all she could do to not shout at him. His lack of attention was very tiresome. "Miss Catherine Hayward will be here on Sunday afternoon."

"Good. I'll expect her then."

"I don't suppose I shall see you at Norfolk House tomorrow night?" She wondered if he dare attend another party and risk being compromised. His marital status was certainly more important to him than a few hours spent in male camaraderie and turns on the dance floor with a handful of beautiful young ladies.

Robert followed his mother to the foyer. "I dare not show my face until my chaperone arrives."

Oh yes, the Duchess knew they pursued him—for his title, for his income, and for the exquisitely handsome man himself. She smiled and patted her son's cheek. "Dear, it's not your *face* I worry about."

At two in the afternoon on Sunday, Catherine climbed into the crested carriage and settled in the corner, across from the Duchess of Waverly. Her Grace signaled the driver to depart.

Catherine dabbed her moist eyes.

The Duchess touched Catherine's arm. "I can see it was an emotional farewell."

"Yes, it was." The two oldest Talbot children were brave, barely shedding a tear. However, Tommy had clung to her leg, refusing to let his beloved governess leave, screaming, "Don't go," at the top of his lungs. Catherine would never forget the look in adorable Chloe's eyes.

She thought about how overseeing a grown man would be different than minding children. A stern, disapproving glance would surely not bring an end to his petulant behavior. Could she employ a hug and a kiss to mend his skinned knee or his hurt feelings? Catherine could safely guarantee she would never see the Marquess groveling on the floor, as the children had, to cure what ailed him.

Catherine gave a final sniff and tucked her handkerchief in her reticule. "I do, however, feel very uncertain about my new position."

"The only issue I foresee is acceptance within society." The Duchess' face remained impassive as she stared out the window. "The *ton* can be very unforgiving in their ways."

Employment as a man's chaperone sounded peculiar at best. Would the opinion of others really matter?

"I believe Haverton's position holds some weight. I cannot help but assume"—the Duchess looked at Catherine—"you will not encounter any difficulties."

"I hope not. It has been a very long time since I attended any social functions, none ever in Town. I am not sure that I will know what to do."

"Do not worry, I'm sure you will learn of his expectations soon enough. He's very good at letting his wishes be known, you know. I am his mother and cannot help but think of him as a dear, dear boy, but a trifle on the self-absorbed side, I'm afraid."

Catherine bit her lower lip to keep from laughing.

"I am glad that amuses you, my dear. As bad a time as Haverton says he has with the ladies, he has a fine sense of humor about it himself and finds his popularity equally as humorous—but he grows weary of the constant pursuit.

"The problem is everything comes much too easy for him. He hasn't had to work for a thing. He was born with exceptional looks and he will inherit the title of duke. We need not mention his wealth. I must admit his manners are exemplary," the Duchess related with pride. "I am quite sure he could charm the stars from the sky if he put his mind to it."

It wouldn't have surprised Catherine to discover the Marquess had wall eyes and a beak for a nose. Mothers always saw the best in their children. She had seen that firsthand with Lady Talbot.

The Duchess' eyebrows rose. "I can see you doubt me."

"I do not mean any disrespect. But to be honest, it is just I find all this praise for your son . . . his lordship, a bit . . . much." She did her best to subdue her smile and regarded the Duchess' devotion as motherly pride. Truly, Catherine just could not imagine any of what Her Grace said to be true.

"I insist we both be completely honest. It is best you

say exactly what is on your mind . . . no secrets here," the Duchess assured her. "Oh yes, you may have your doubts now but you shall see. My son's efforts to hire a chaperone for himself are not due to vanity. I can say that much for him, he has not underestimated his desirability to the opposite sex. They have proved very troublesome for him."

As difficult as Catherine found it to believe, it was enough that the Duchess and the Marquess believed it to be the truth. She gazed down at her reticule and responded, "If you say so, Your Grace."

The Waverly carriage rolled to a stop at Moreland Manor. The Duchess instructed the footmen to take Catherine's luggage to her rooms.

"Come, let me introduce you to my son." She strode through the entrance hall with Catherine not far behind. "I believe we shall find him in his study." She paused and whispered to Catherine. "Next to his evenings out, he finds pleasure in keeping orderly books. He constantly has a pencil to paper."

Just as the Duchess had suspected, there sat Robert in his shirt sleeves among an assortment of papers. He looked up from his work and shuffled the papers, clearly hiding his current piece of work. "Mother, you're here."

"I have brought her, your new chaperone." The Duchess held her hand out for Catherine to come forward so he might see her. "This is Miss Catherine Hayward."

He acknowledged her with a mumble while still sitting at his desk.

Why didn't he have the decency to stand when they entered the room? He wasn't making a favorable impression at all. That's what comes of being so lenient with him when he was a boy.

The butler appeared in the hallway.

"Maybury," the Duchess said over her shoulder. "Show Miss Hayward to the drawing room. We'll have tea there."

"Yes, Your Grace." The butler motioned to Catherine. "This way please, miss." She followed him down the hall.

"We're to take tea then I'm going to see that Miss Hayward is properly settled."

"Very good, Mother." Robert shuffled the papers, continuing to cover some document he did not wish her to see in front of him.

"You will be joining us, won't you?"

"I do not believe so." Something on the desk seemed to be luring his attention.

What could be so important? "That is a shame," she replied with as much displeasure as she could manage. "How will you two ever become acquainted?"

Robert looked up from his papers. "I promise I shall have a word with her before we attend the Trowbridge's soiree tonight."

"So you are to attend?" At least he planned to take advantage of his new chaperone and go out for the evening.

"Will you not be there?"

This was the first time he showed more than a passing interest in what she said. "I am afraid not. I've another engagement to attend. You must tell me how she works out."

"I am rather anxious to see what comes of it myself."

"I imagine there will be several disappointed ladies." After tonight, the Duchess mused, London will never be the same again.

Chapter Three

The Duchess of Waverly had not been exaggerating about her son's appearance. Catherine stepped into the drawing room and exhaled. Lord Haverton could be described only as absolutely *beautiful*.

Handsome, she corrected herself. Men were handsome, ladies were beautiful. But neither word was adequate to describe her new employer. He was beyond mere handsome. He far surpassed the picture the Duchess had painted of him.

Did his mother really think he could charm the stars from the sky? From what Catherine could see, the Marquess had the personality of a schoolroom chalkboard.

But she could now understand why he needed a chaperone. Lord Haverton's facial features were chiseled from marble, crafted by artistic skill, every angle perfectly formed, each plane of his face flawless. His dark, thick hair would make any woman envious. He was no less than perfection itself.

Catherine had only seen him sitting behind his desk. If his broad shoulders were any indication of the rest of his physique, "desirable" would also be an insufficient word to describe him. Should he have been out of sorts and Her Grace's description of his manners correct, that would certainly make Lord Haverton the most sought-after man in London.

If his character were to equal his looks, this man would be a lethal combination for any woman. She would surely melt while under the penetrating gaze of his dark brown eyes. Just the thought of living under the same roof with that wonderfully handsome man made her heart quicken.

She wondered if he had any intention of engaging her affections and plunged into her reticule for her spectacles. Lady Talbot had told Catherine more than once she was *pretty*. And being *pretty* could be dangerous in London. She slipped on her spectacles. Catherine did not want him to show interest in her of any kind. She pushed the glasses toward the bridge of her nose, never doubting that her bluestocking appearance would discourage any man's advances.

The Duchess paused in the doorway of the drawing room before entering. Miss Hayward stared aimlessly into the room. Adrift in her own thoughts, the Duchess supposed. *The girl has had only one look at Robert and was already lost, although she might not know it yet.*

"I must apologize for my son. I'm afraid we've caught him in the midst of his work. It is not particularly a good time."

Catherine turned to face Her Grace. "I'll note that for future reference."

"He becomes quite distracted—sometimes he appears almost thick!" The Duchess took a cleansing breath and continued. "He has informed me that he wishes to give you a twenty pound advance." She looked up when Catherine gasped. "You'll need to purchase matching gloves and shoes for your new gowns."

"New gowns?"

She had to proceed with caution. The Duchess did not wish to make the position sound too good to be true. "Your current gowns are fine for the schoolroom but they will not do for the Assembly. And, of course, he will be paying for the new gowns."

"I beg your pardon? Did you say his lordship would be paying for my new gowns?"

"Oh, yes." Her Grace nodded. "He was very insistent on that point."

The housekeeper arrived with the tea. The Duchess sent her away, stating she would pour out. "I'm afraid you'll have to make do with what you have for tonight."

"Tonight?" Catherine leaned forward, sitting up

straighter and more wide-eyed. "Are we to go out to-night?"

"You shall accompany Haverton to the Trowbridge soiree." The Duchess set her gloves and reticule aside and lifted the teapot.

"It is my duty. I suppose I must." Catherine eased back into the sofa, accepting her new responsibility. "I cannot possibly refuse."

"Good. I'll see to it, personally, that you have what you need. I shall come by tomorrow morning and take you to my modiste."

"I thank you, Your Grace. You are most generous. I'm afraid I should not know where to begin."

"I shall not abandon you now. I will keep in close contact until you are comfortably installed. You may rely on that."

"I do not know what to say." A mixture of gratitude and relief shone in her eyes. "You are too kind."

"Think nothing of it. My son feels he needs you for his protection. Moreland Manor will be your new home until the time the Marquess finds just the right young woman to become his wife."

After tea, Her Grace led Catherine to the gold suite abovestairs and pushed open the large door. "I hope this will be adequate." The Duchess swept into the first room.

"Adequate?" Catherine entered. She had never seen

such apartments in her life and doubted Lord and Lady Talbot inhabited such lush quarters. "Is all this for me?"

"Yes, it is. Haverton told me himself that you should have the very best."

Catherine looked at the high ceiling and white walls decorated with intricate patterns of gold leaf. Beyond the open doors on the right lay the bedchamber. "I cannot help but think there is something more to all this."

"I'm afraid you do not comprehend the importance of your position. Tonight you shall see for yourself. Do allow me to have a look at your gowns. I'll have a better idea what we should purchase tomorrow."

Catherine followed the Duchess through the bedchamber to the dressing room on the far side. Her meager wardrobe couldn't fill a corner of the massive closet.

"Oh, dear." Her Grace skimmed through the gowns. "You shall need more than just a few."

"What shall I do about tonight? Do I have anything suitable to wear?"

"Tonight? Let me see." The Duchess returned to the beginning of the rack for a second look. "This might do." She pulled out a light blue gown and held it out for further inspection. "It's very modest but it will definitely suffice."

Catherine took the dress and draped it over her arm.

"It's time I be on my way." The Duchess pulled on her gloves and headed for the door.

"Thank you for everything, Your Grace." She trailed behind the Duchess. "You have been more than kind."

"Do not give it another thought, my dear. I shall see you tomorrow and you can tell me everything that transpired at tonight's party." At the doorway, Her Grace paused and turned back toward Catherine. "I expect Haverton will have a word with you presently."

Presently arrived a half hour later. Catherine stood at the doorway to the drawing room and had a good, long look at her new employer.

Lord Haverton stood with his arms crossed, posture-perfect straight, as if posing for a portrait. His eyes were open wide, staring out the picture window. He was taller than she had expected. At least he had the decency to dress properly before meeting with her. He wore a jacket of forest green over the shirt she had seen him in earlier. Fawn breeches stretched over the upper part of his long legs and his exquisitely polished top boots were much to be admired.

Catherine cleared her throat. "You sent for me, my lord?"

The Marquess turned from the window. "Ah, yes—if you would please be seated, *Mrs. Hayes*." He gestured to the sofa for her to sit but he remained standing.

"I beg your pardon, but it is *Hayward*, your lordship. *Miss* Hayward," Catherine corrected and sat as he instructed. How could he have been so completely wrong regarding her name?

"Yes, of course it is," he said, clearly distracted as he rubbed his chin between his thumb and forefinger. "This is dashed peculiar. My mother has informed me she explained about the particulars, such as your wages and living arrangements."

"Yes, she has."

"I believe all there is left to speak to you about are your duties." Lord Haverton paced back toward the window. "It has been my personal observation that most ladies' chaperones fail in their responsibility to properly oversee their wards.

"Thus I find it imperative that I provide a chaperone for these ladies. That is where you come in. I expect that you should watch for unseemly behavior. Nothing suspect should transpire between myself and any lady in my company. There should be no question about the propriety of our exchange."

"I quite understand."

"I'm sure you will find my manners exemplary. I'm afraid I cannot speak as well for the ladies. In some cases, they may prove to exhibit less than ladylike behavior."

"I believe I understand completely, my lord." If any other man except this one before her had said he needed a chaperone to ward off women, Catherine would have disgraced herself by laughing out loud. But in Lord Haverton's case she feared what he said could very well be true.

"Well then, if everything is settled, I am attending

the Trowbridge soiree tonight. I trust you will not keep me waiting? I wish to leave by eight."

"As you say, my lord, eight o'clock."

Three hours after her arrival at Moreland Manor, Catherine had settled in and was partaking of a light supper in the privacy of her sitting room on the orders of her employer.

He, Lord Haverton, was not to be seen. Did he eat? Would she see him before they departed for the evening? Catherine was looking very forward to their next meeting. He could not possibly be as she remembered him . . . as *handsome* as she remembered.

No, impossible.

Not long after finishing her meal, she began her toilette.

Other than changing her dress, Catherine did nothing to alter her appearance. She inspected herself in the pier glass. She wore her blue, high-collared dress. The dress the Duchess thought modest was in fact Catherine's finest. She coiled her hair into the same tight bun she always wore atop her head and slid her spectacles in place. She was ready.

"Honoria, I will not allow the opportunity of the Marquess of Haverton to slip by." Lady Darlington glared with determination at her daughter's reflection in the dressing glass. "I want you to throw yourself straight into his arms!"

"But Mama, I do not think I could do as you ask."

"Fustian! You are the loveliest young lady London has to offer. I would not be shocked if you were the Incomparable of the Season."

Honoria turned from the glass and pulled out of her mother's tight grasp. "But I only want to marry for love, Mama."

"Hush! Ridiculous notion. You will do as you're told," Lady Darlington ordered. "Now remember, if he reaches for you, you will go straight into his arms."

Honoria shook her head and remained mute.

"If he kisses you, you will act as if you have soared to the heights of heaven." Lady Darlington stretched her hand out and upward, illustrating the lengths she wanted her daughter to ascend.

Honoria sniveled.

"And if he wishes to do anything more"—Lady Darlington paused, deciding against an explanation of exactly what the *more* would entail—"you will willingly allow him that liberty too."

Honoria's banked tears flowed. Where was the girl's backbone? No doubt her weakness came from her father. Lady Darlington fingered a ringlet of her daughter's hair, setting it back in place.

"Yes, you will, my dear girl. You shall do as you're told and your mama will see that everything works out as planned. We shall wait until Haverton grows tired of the crowd. He can only tolerate the flock of women for so long before he requires solitude to recuperate. That is when we shall make our move."

"Must we, Mama?" Honoria whimpered. "I do not know if I can go through with it."

"You will. You most certainly will." Lady Darlington could envision the Marquess moving away from the ladies to find momentary companionship with his gentleman friends, Lord Fitzgerald and Sir Giles Winthrop.

It wouldn't be long after that, she thought. He'd most likely dance two sets and remove himself for a quarter of an hour or so. It was a pattern, she noted, that he repeated. And because of that predictable behavior, Lady Darlington would snare her lovely Honoria the most eligible bachelor in England.

Dressed in her blue gown, Catherine waited in the drawing room of Moreland Manor at two minutes before eight. She adjusted her spectacles and ran her hand over her head, finding not one hair had strayed from her tight bun. She was not about to be tardy for her first outing with the Marquess.

After five minutes had passed, an immaculately dressed Lord Haverton, sporting a black jacket over a pair of white satin knee breeches and a snowy white cravat, stepped into the room. "Come, *Mrs. Hayes*, it is time to be on our way," he announced without preamble.

"*Miss Hayward*, your lordship." Catherine was nearly past the point of correcting him. Not that it mattered, but for one reason or another he simply could not remember her name.

"Yes, of course it is." Absorbed in the task of pulling on his gloves, Lord Haverton never looked up.

How could Catherine have ever thought he had any interest in her? Goodness, he could not even remember her name.

The butler opened the front door and Catherine pulled her wrap about her while the Marquess headed straight for the waiting carriage. Without hesitation, he entered and Catherine, after his lordship had settled, followed discreetly behind.

During the trip, Lord Haverton never spoke to her, never looked at her and never in any way acknowledged her presence. Catherine might as well have been invisible. Better that he not notice her than take interest in her, she thought.

Music from the Trowbridge residence spilled into the streets upon their arrival. Stepping out of the coach, she glanced over the top of her spectacles, marveling at the line of carriages and the splendor of the house stretched out before her.

Upon entering, Lord Haverton paused at the top of the stairs, gazing down on the room where the guests congregated. "Mrs. Hayes," he said over his shoulder.

Catherine moved forward, closing the distance between them. "Yes, my lord?"

"Remember, you are to keep careful watch over me. If I should leave the room, I expect you to follow directly."

"Understood, your lordship." Only when she followed him into the Trowbridge's grand saloon did Catherine understand why.

Glancing over the rims of her spectacles, she watched the Marquess until he descended the stairs and moved partially out of her sight.

A sea of women stopped and parted to face him when he reached ground level. As he approached, line after line of women curtsied, sending a rippling effect to the back of the room. Catherine would not have believed it if she hadn't seen it for herself.

Lord Haverton bowed his head, greeting the ladies on either side of him. He stopped and bent to the ground. Rising, the Marquess held out a red-tasseled, ivory fan, returning it to its owner.

A small, delicate gloved hand reached out and grasped the proffered fan. "Thank you, my lord." A quite lovely young lady in white with a pale green overskirt dropped into a deep curtsy and proffered a shy smile.

Catherine removed her reading glasses and slipped them into her reticule. There was certainly no need for them. How silly of her to think the Marquess of Haverton would ever notice her when he had his choice of all these breathtakingly beautiful ladies.

Instead of the great blur of light shining from above, Catherine could see the details of the large crystal chandelier, flooding the room with light. Down below, the lavishly dressed guests and bejeweled lords and ladies dripped with gemstones of every imaginable color.

Catherine had never seen such splendor. Even her grandfather's manor had not been host to a gathering such as this.

The next several hours resulted in a countless number of recklessly tossed fans tumbling to the floor. Each time Lord Haverton retrieved the wayward item with patient gallantry. He stood up for only a few dances. To break the monotony of retrieving fans, Catherine joked to herself.

As of yet, she had not been needed and had sat with the dowagers and other chaperones in a corner. Even they did not seem to notice her. They looked on, watching the couples on the dance floor and whispering, commenting to each other.

Three chaperones stood only a few feet away. She had not intended to eavesdrop but heard Lord Haverton's name as the topic of their conversation.

"The Marquess of Haverton has gone beyond the pale," one of the women said.

"Who would not forgive the Handsome Haverton anything?" a short, red-haired lady standing next to the first asked.

"What's he done now, Miss Trueblood?" a third interceded, ignoring the red-haired woman.

"He has installed a young woman at Moreland Manor, Miss Price," the one named Miss Trueblood announced. "For what purpose one can only guess."

The red-hair woman gasped. "He cannot possibly have—"

"Oh yes, Mrs. Baldwin, it is true. I had it of Mrs. Brooks, Lady Stratton's lady's maid."

Moved into Moreland Manor? Catherine had just moved in—could they possibly be talking about her?

"It was only a matter of time." By the tone of Miss Price's voice, she had expected something along these lines to occur.

"It's positively scandalous!" Mrs. Baldwin said.

"In his own home?" Miss Price exclaimed, clearly shocked beyond belief. "Utterly unimaginable."

The ladies could not have been talking about her, could they? Good sense prevailed and Catherine held her tongue. Her job was not to correct wayward gossip, but to protect the reputation of her employer, even if the malicious gossip was about *her* and him. *Gossip*, she reminded herself, was harmless.

The thought of him, Lord Haverton . . . the very idea that he or she—that they might engage in anything improper . . . Catherine felt the flush of warmth creep up her cheeks. What these ladies were insinuating was so very far from the truth. She was his chaperone and nothing more. For heaven's sake, he couldn't even recall her name.

"And as you can see for yourselves"—Miss Trueblood gestured to the dance floor before her—"he has the attention of every lady in attendance, if not the entire Town."

Mrs. Baldwin shrugged. "Why does one man need so many women?"

Miss Price and Miss Trueblood glared at the third of their trio whose face had turned as scarlet as her hair.

"Some men are simply not satisfied with one woman," Miss Price enlightened the red-haired Mrs. Baldwin.

She pressed her palm to the base of her throat. "Not my Lord Haverton—"

The truth was, Catherine noted, catching a glimpse of him on the dance floor, Lord Haverton seemed especially careful not to pay too much attention to any one lady in particular. He had danced his first set with a blond and this set with a dark-haired beauty.

"I see it is not only the young chits who make a cake of themselves over him." Miss Trueblood gave Mrs. Baldwin a scathing look. "Would you wish yourself twenty years younger so you could compete for a fraction of his attention? Drop a fan at his feet, perhaps?"

"For him to notice me, I'd need to be thirty years younger." Mrs. Baldwin laughed. "And he half-blind."

"You are naughty," Miss Price scolded but laughed in good humor.

"I fear it would take more than beauty to gain his favor," Miss Trueblood said with her gaze firmly fixed on the Marquess, studying him.

"You know, Miss Trueblood," Miss Price countered, "I believe you are right. It will take more than mere beauty to interest *that* man."

The music had come to an end. Haverton bowed to his partner. She was lovely, he noted, and quite pleas-

ant to dance with, as were all the ladies he had partnered, but it was time to retreat. He returned Miss Darrow to her chaperone, bowed over her hand, and
excused himself.

Tonight he need not give a second thought whether
he ought not try to find solitude or if his actions would
chance another questionable encounter. For once, he
simply could do as he wished. Escaping the stifling heat
of the ballroom, the Marquess stepped through the guests
milling about on the dance floor and beyond the room,
into the back garden for a breath of air.

So far, the evening had gone well. Uneventful but the
night was still young. Something would transpire before the evening came to an end. He had no doubt at all.

"Lord Haverton?" came the soft, sultry, feminine
voice. A slender, tempting silhouette stepped out from
the shadows. It wasn't one he recognized.

"Whom do I have the pleasure of addressing?" He
tried to discern any distinguishing characteristics that
might help him identify his company.

"Is that really so important?" She turned to the right,
looking away from him. "We have not, as of yet, been
properly introduced. However, I believe we could become very well acquainted."

Haverton glanced to his left, wondering what . . . or
perhaps who, she looked at. One could not guarantee
privacy in an outdoor area, he thought. It would not do
at all to be caught, but she . . . whoever she was, was so

very intriguing. And with his chaperone ready to intervene in a thrice, he could allow this scene to play out—perhaps even enjoying himself.

The Grace with which she moved, the lilting voice and the soft, pleasant scent, were factors working together, convincing him to remain in her company. He need not worry about leaping out a window or into a fountain to escape when the time came.

After all, was he not a man? Haverton stepped toward her and she moved back, her feet skidded across the flagstone in quick, nervous retreat.

Interesting . . . what was she playing at? Her words might have suggested an invitation but her actions told Haverton otherwise.

Go on—go on, Honoria, Lady Darlington urged silently from her darkened corner. She had told her daughter to be forthright, daring, and bold!

What was her daughter waiting for? All the girl had to do was embrace him. In turn, he would embrace her. Discovering the couple in a kiss would not hurt their cause either.

An innocent young lady on her first year out, such as her Honoria, would certainly fall victim to a known roué such as Haverton. Lady Darlington would step out and catch him—them together—and the deed would be done.

"Go on, Honoria, go on," Lady Darlington whispered.

Honoria stepped forward—finally. *Yes, that's it.* She held out her hand, reaching for the Marquess.

"That's it, that's it." *Take hold of his coat lapel, just as I told you, then slide your hand around his neck.* "Closer, now, closer—"

Someone stepped toward the couple from the far side of the courtyard. "I beg your pardon." It was a woman.

Honoria drew away from Lord Haverton and stepped back.

"Excuse me," a woman's voice interrupted. "I'm afraid I must ask that if you wish to converse with his lordship, young lady, you should do so from a distance."

Who was she? Lady Darlington's chest tightened. Who was this . . . this . . . intruder? Just when Honoria was making progress!

Honoria broke into tears and fled toward the house, burying her face in her hands.

Lady Darlington nearly stepped out of her hiding place and pushed that hussy back into the ballroom.

"Pity, don't know who that young woman was," Haverton said to the unwelcome woman. "But she was a fetching thing."

"Have I acted improperly, my lord?"

"No, Mrs. Hayes. You have done precisely what I had wished."

Mrs. Hayes? What Lady Darlington could not fathom was *what* was Mrs. Hayes doing here? And *who*, exactly, she was.

The Marquess peered around the garden. Catherine followed the path of Lord Haverton's gaze around the darkened perimeter.

"Unless I miss my guess, her mother is hiding somewhere, standing ready to pounce when the moment proved right," he said.

The man was simply too much. Did he really think women were lying in wait for him? Or looking at him as the prize to be won?

"Mrs. Hayes, I believe I've had enough fresh air for the time being. Let us join the other guests, shall we?"

Catherine followed Haverton into the house. She stopped before entering and made a final scan of the shadows surrounding the garden. A movement caught her attention. Was it the turn of a leaf in the gentle breeze? Perhaps the scurry of a rodent? Or was there truly someone out there hiding?

Entering the ballroom, the Marquess met his companions Sir Giles, Lord Fitzgerald, and Mr. Brewster where he had left them earlier.

"What's going on out there, Haverton?" Sir Giles gave a half-interested glance out the French doors. "A young girl's just run through here like the hounds were after her."

"Another near miss, I'm afraid." Haverton straightened the cuffs of his shirt.

Fitzgerald looked over Haverton's jacket. "You don't appear to have damaged your coat—and you have managed to keep from climbing into the trees." He lifted the Marquess' arm, checking on the condition of his coat sleeve.

"You're dry," Brewster told the surrounding gentlemen. "You missed hiding out in the fountain. How'd you manage to escape this time around?"

"I would have at least expected you to scale the wall and catch the seat of your pants on the brambles." Sir Giles stole a look at Haverton's backside.

"Quite simply"—Haverton smoothed his evening coat, hoping to indicate that nothing of the kind had happened—"the chaperone intervened."

"Do you mean the young lady's chaperone stood there and allowed you to—"

"No, *my* chaperone."

"Yours?" Brewster said wide-eyed and open-mouthed. Fitzgerald and Sir Giles broke out into wild laughter. "You did say *your* chaperone, did you not, Haverton?"

"You are correct." He proudly displayed a smug smile. "I most definitely did."

"Gad! I'd never thought I'd see the day." Sir Giles wiped the tears from his eyes with a dark blue silk handkerchief. "A *man* with a chaperone!"

"You've outdone yourself this time." Fitzgerald clapped Haverton on the back, more strongly than was necessary.

By this time the whole roomful of guests were laughing. The word had spread toward the back of the room that the Marquess of Haverton had a chaperone for himself.

"She has worked out splendidly," the Marquess concluded.

Sir Giles had stopped laughing and considered the

matter with a great deal of seriousness. "That's a dashed clever idea. Puts an end to all that 'compromising position' business, don't it?"

It most certainly had.

"Should have thought of it myself," Fitzgerald commented to Brewster next to him. "Bang up idea."

Brewster chuckled, marveling at the Marquess' ingenuity. "Trust Haverton to come up with something so foolproof."

"So simple!" Sir Giles stood between Brewster and Fitzgerald, and clapped his arms around each. "Gentlemen, times are changing . . . it is the dawning of a new age . . . the age of man—the bachelor."

Brewster and Fitzgerald cheered. Haverton remained quiet. Among the three of them, more than enough was being said.

"Please . . . please . . ." Sir Giles hushed them and continued. "After tonight most ladies of London will grieve of their loss. Not only will they fail to legshackle a man—he's robbed them of the very opportunity to try."

The Marquess glanced skyward when another round of cheering ensued.

"When my Lord Haverton weds—"

Brewster and Fitzgerald groaned in protest.

"Oh, yes," Sir Giles admitted. "For we know that one day he must . . . we can feel confident it was a deed done of his choosing, not because he's been discovered in the arms of a wily, undesirable miss. Gentlemen, we can say, with full confidence, that the Marquess of Haverton will never fall victim to a parson's mousetrap as an unwilling groom."

Chapter Four

Haverton had a devil of a time prying himself away from his companions. Tolerating attention and admiration from females was one thing, being worshipped by one's contemporaries was quite another.

"There you are, Robert." It was well past one in the morning when Simon came across him in the ballroom. "I've heard the most outrageous thing—too outrageous, even for you."

"And what news is that?" Haverton had no doubt his brother would take his turn and ridicule him for the foolishness of hiring a chaperone. He pointed to something on his brother's shoulder. "What have you here?"

Simon brushed at some small, white petals from his jacket. "Oh, that's nothing."

"Been cornering some chit, I see." Haverton knew the

telltale signs of a tryst and he found this unusual behavior for Simon. His brother was a flirt, not a conqueror.

"Just making her acquaintance." Simon's cheeks reddened. Unlike Haverton, Simon was a bit on the shy side and not used to female attention.

"More than just an acquaintance, I gather." Haverton drew a short three-leafed twig from Simon's hair.

"You're changing the subject," he protested.

"What subject?"

"From the extraordinary news I've heard—" He paused and smiled politely past Haverton. "Excuse me." Simon turned from his brother and gave a shallow bow to Catherine. He smiled and held out his hand. "I don't think I've had the pleasure."

"Are you referring to my chaperone?"

Simon blinked, regarding the woman in disbelief. "I had heard you have gone beyond the pale yet again, but—a chaperone? I say, Robert, that *is* a fresh idea." It didn't take long for Simon to put the pieces together. "Is this what you wanted to speak to Mother about?"

"Simon, this is my chaperone, Mrs. Hayes." Haverton brought her forward with a gesture. "Mrs. Hayes, my brother, Lord Simon."

Catherine curtsied. "It is an honor, Lord Simon."

"Mrs. Hayes"—Lord Moreland bowed over her hand—"I must admit it is more of a shock than a pleasure."

"That is quite understandable, sir."

"Now that we have dispensed with the introductions,

I believe I shall circulate among the guests," Haverton announced. "Mrs. Hayes, I suggest you rejoin the rest of the chaperones and continue your vigilance until I am in further need of your presence."

"Yes, my lord." Catherine headed for the chaperone corner.

Lord Simon did not follow his brother. "Are you coming, Simon?"

"I'll be with you presently." Simon called out, "Mrs. Hayes, a moment, please."

Catherine paused, waiting for Lord Simon. Although handsome in his own right, he was not quite as devastatingly handsome as his brother.

Lord Simon leaned forward and she did the same, keeping their conversation quiet and assuring privacy. "Tell me, Mrs. Hayes, are you truly my brother's chaperone? Or is this all a hum?"

Miss Hayward. Catherine almost corrected him but decided against it. The second thing to occur to Catherine was that Lord Simon looked *at* her, and spoke *to* her, not just in her general direction as her employer had.

How many more times would she need to confirm or explain her position? "Yes, as unusual as it may sound, I am Lord Haverton's chaperone."

"If anyone can change the constraints of London society, he will certainly be the one to do it, all right."

"I doubt the Marquess intends this arrangement to go as far as that." Catherine kept an eye on her charge who stood across the room.

"Don't be surprised if you're not the only gentlemen's chaperone after the night is out. I might venture to say it won't take long before your arrangement will be considered *de rigueur* and adapted by other members of the *ton*."

"And what of his lordship's brother?" Catherine wondered if he would give in and do the very same. "What happens to you, my lord, for consorting with the likes of a chaperone?"

"Me?" Lord Simon splayed a hand upon his chest. "I am the mere younger son of a duke. I need not make an impression nor amount to much when all is said and done."

This young man appeared to Catherine to have his feet solidly planted on the ground, at least more so than his brother. Lord Simon had none of the airs that the rest of society displayed.

"Did my mother talk you into this?" Lord Simon murmured with a pretense of scratching the tip of his nose.

"She was the one who recommended me for this position, yes."

"I should have known she would have had a part in all this. I can't imagine what you thought when she told you that you were to be a chaperone for a man."

Lord Simon's chuckle turned into full-fledged laughter. Apparently he possessed a very good imagination.

"Just the thought of him in danger of being compromised." He couldn't stop laughing. "That a woman would purposely—I mean, a lady would have to—have to—" He stopped, the smile faded from his lips and he cleared his throat before turning scarlet. "I do beg your pardon."

Catherine tried to give him a reassuring smile. "I must admit, I, too, was skeptical at first but after what I have observed in the garden just this evening . . . well, I suppose the biggest shock is it would appear that Lord Haverton does, after all, require a chaperone."

Lady Darlington stalked to her daughter's room several hours later. She had mopped away her tears of anger, humiliation, and failure. Tears she did not wish Honoria to see. "He most certainly has made a laughingstock out of us all!"

How would she combat such outmaneuvering? A chaperone—*his* chaperone was completely unexpected. Who ever would have thought it was a possibility?

She'd find a way, Lady Darlington vowed. It might take a while but she would find a way around Lord Haverton's chaperone.

It was by some stroke of luck that no one had recognized Honoria when she ran through the crowded ballroom. That discovery might have proved to be unfortunate.

Lady Darlington tucked her handkerchief into her sleeve. With staunch determination, she vowed that she would not be thwarted again. Before the Season was out, Honoria would have him.

Honoria sat calm and wide-eyed in front of her dressing table mirror, staring into the middle of the room, without the usual trembling when her mother ranted. It was a most unsatisfactory reaction. Lady Darlington arched an inquisitive brow, wondering what could possibly be going through her daughter's head.

"You don't seem to have been troubled one way or the other, my dear," she said in a much softer, cloying tone.

Honoria sighed. Along with the dreamy quality of her eyes, it was the gentle expression of a smitten young lady. "He was a most . . . agreeable gentleman."

Relief swept through Lady Darlington. Half the battle was already won. If Honoria had accepted him, everything would fall into place. "Of course he is amiable. Did I not tell you? Every woman in Town desires him!"

Honoria smiled, and exhaled slowly in contentment. What was going on with the girl? Her behavior was most peculiar.

"Why don't you go to bed, dear?" Lady Darlington gave her daughter's arm a loving squeeze. What's this? A twig? With a small, white bloom. She must have snagged a bush on her way into the house, after Haverton's woman had intruded.

Lady Darlington didn't need to be reminded of the failure of tonight's plan. She crushed the twig in her hand.

Oh! The shame!

* * *

The Duchess of Waverly stood in the front parlor of Moreland Manor and watched her son come to an undignified, abrupt halt in the hallway. Dressed in a fine Hunter green morning coat and tan pantaloons, Robert made the detour in her direction.

"Mother, whatever are you doing here? I hadn't expected to see you today."

"Aren't you glad to see your mother?" she returned, rather pointedly. The Duchess wasn't sure if she was to be pleased or cross with her eldest today.

"It is *always* a delight to see you, you know that." He took her hands in both of his and greeted her with a kiss on each cheek.

"Oh, save it for someone who'll believe it, Robert. Your charm is useless on me."

Without a word, he led the way to the sofa and invited her to sit. "Shall I send for some tea?"

She settled onto the sofa and replied, "No, dear. I'm not here to see you." As much as she loved him, the Duchess knew her son believed the world revolved about him. "Miss Hayward is expecting me."

"Who?" The momentary confusion on his face cleared.

"Your chaperone." The Duchess could hardly wait to hear what went on last night. She wanted to know what Catherine thought of Robert and how society had received her presence.

"Yes, of course," he replied in that tone the Duchess

recognized as one of noncompliance. She knew not to press him further.

She leveled a discerning gaze at her son. Although Robert would have something to say regarding his chaperone, the Duchess was certain she would not get a clear answer to what he thought of Catherine.

"I am to take her for new gowns this afternoon," the Duchess announced. No need for her to repeat that he would be receiving the bills. When they arrived, he'd remember well enough.

Robert squeezed his eyes closed, adding to his expression of disapproval.

"Don't be so clutch-fisted." She slapped him on the shoulder. "You can well afford it."

"It's not the blunt, mother. It's—"

"If you hire a lady, you must expect to assume all expenses of employing that lady. I should think you more than anyone would know that. I know what goes on in Town, you know. I don't bury my head in the country like your father." She pointed in the general direction of Suffolk. "Now tell me, how was the Trowbridge soiree last night? And what of Miss Hayward, dear?"

"Couldn't have gone better. I should have done this years ago. Employing a chaperone has proven to be a complete success. Unfortunately, I seem to have drawn much more interest with her than I would have expected."

The Duchess returned a look of disapproval. "I am

not asking about the performance of her duties. I am speaking about Miss Hayward, herself."

Clearly she had surprised Robert. He was, if she were to believe what she saw, speechless.

"Honestly, you have more hair than wit," she announced in no uncertain terms.

Robert's eyes widened and his jaw dropped open.

She cut off any protest by immediately continuing. "Just like your father. I gave birth to you. I should know if you're a ninny."

"I am not accustomed to being spoken to in that manner, not even by my mother," he managed after her stupefying words.

"Get used to it! If you're going to act as if you haven't a brain in your head, you might as well be treated as such."

Robert stood and rubbed his forehead. "Mother . . . what *are* you going on about?"

"Your chaperone, of course. Have you not paid her any attention?"

"Of course I've noticed her. I breakfasted with her just this morning. She accompanied me last evening to the Trowbridge do. How could I not have noticed her?"

The Duchess pursed her lips in concentration. She hated to be the one who caused the smooth, handsome forehead of his to wrinkle. But he simply had to learn to pay attention.

"I doubt you would notice your own nose except it is stuck between your eyes. Only the good Lord knows what would have happened if he saw fit to place it on the back of your head."

Robert's puzzled expression deepened. "Why would my nose be on the back of my head?"

"That is not the point!"

"Mother, you are making it quite difficult to follow this conversation."

Trying to keep her patience, the Duchess leaned back, closed her eyes and regained her composure. "All right, then, tell me exactly how old do you think Miss Hayward is?"

"How old? Do you mean her age?"

"Yes, dear, her age." The Duchess gazed at him with great concern. Perhaps placing Catherine under foot was not close enough for him to take notice.

Robert rubbed his chin. One would think he was puzzling strategy for the war instead of stating his opinion. "I haven't given it a thought, really."

"Humor this old woman and do so now."

"Mother, I really don't know," Robert replied with equal impatience. "I never thought to inquire."

"Inquire? How impertinent! You do not ask a lady her age. Have you no sense at all?"

Although weak, he attempted a reply.

Again the Duchess cut him off. "To notice would mean you would have to *see* her, look *at* her." She could have well imagined he had spent all that time in Catherine's company and not taken any notice of her.

"Certainly I've looked at her, Mother."

"Really . . ." She bobbed her head, waiting for him to elaborate. He didn't and she asked, "What color is her hair would you say?"

"Her hair? Well . . . let me see . . ." If he did not answer these questions correctly, Haverton knew serious trouble loomed ahead. "Let me see . . ." He tried to think of something to say. "It's not dark, but it's not light, either."

"Not dark, but not light. What color do you suppose that is, dear?"

"That would make it somewhere in between." His reply sounded weak, even to him.

"How clever of you." She raised her hands to the sky. "I've raised a blessed genius."

He'd botched that one. Her immediate praise obviously meant he had been completely off.

"Since she has this in-between hair color how would you decide her age?"

Mother was going back there, was she? "Well, if I were to hazard a guess."

"Yes?"

"I would have to say that she's not exactly old." What was he going to say? What would appease his mother? If he knew, he'd say almost anything to make her happy. "Nor would I venture to say she was exactly young."

"Not old and not young," the Duchess repeated unamused. "At least you're consistent in your obscure description of your chaperone. One hopes she doesn't get lost because you could never pick her out of a crowd."

"Why on earth would Mrs. Hayes get lost? I assure you I intend to provide transportation—"

The Duchess' blistering glare stopped him in mid-sentence.

Haverton would not be intimidated, not even by his own mother. "I must object at your treatment, Mother. Mrs. Hayes—"

"Her name is *Miss Hayward*!"

"—is little better than a servant. I do not know how old she is, nor do I care, really." He flopped into a chair and sat with both his arms and legs crossed.

"Perhaps you should."

There were certain times such as this when he felt as if he were still ten years old and had never grown up. He stood when his mother rose to greet Mrs. Hayes. The chaperone curtsied and, if Haverton wasn't mistaken, moved not so much toward his mother but more away from him.

"And how are you this morning, Miss Hayward?" The Duchess gave a respectful, wide smile, the impressive one she reserved for those of her rank and above.

"I find that I am more fatigued than usual, Your Grace."

"London parties will do that to you. Are you ready to leave?"

"Yes, Your Grace."

"Let us be on our way then, shall we? You will excuse us, won't you, Robert?" Her Grace gestured Catherine out of the room, and turned back to her son. "Do give serious thought about what we've been discussing, dear."

Sinking into his chair, Robert answered with a groan.

It had been a good ten minutes since the Waverly carriage pulled away from Moreland Manor. The Duchess shifted in her seat and smiled at Catherine, with her usual warmth. "Why is it you allow my son to call you Mrs. Hayes?"

"I'm afraid that correcting him is an endless task."

"He is so stubborn." By Her Grace's expression, Catherine guessed it was a difficulty she had to deal with over the years. "He gets these things into his head." She tapped her own with two fingers. "Where he gets that from, I cannot imagine."

"I don't mind, really. *Mrs. Hayes* sounds more respectable, don't you think? Especially for a chaperone."

The Duchess smiled. "I am glad you are not bothered by his disregard of your proper name." She glanced away for a moment, and whispered, "Perhaps it will all work out better in the end . . ."

"Excuse me?" Catherine hadn't quite caught everything Her Grace had said.

"It's nothing. Tell me how you enjoyed your evening."

In her embarrassment, Catherine studied the twisted strings of her reticule.

"Come now, do not be shy. Remember, you must answer me honestly. There are no set rules for your position therefore we must always be truthful with one another."

Her Grace had the right of it. There was no one in all of England who chaperoned a man. As little as he cared to guide and discuss what should be *proper* conduct, he had not. Catherine was given simple instructions. She actually welcomed the Duchess' intervention in this matter.

"You'll think me quite foolish, Your Grace, but I have never seen such splendor in all my life."

Her Grace lifted her chin, and regarded Catherine through her lowered eyelids. "Was I mistaken about Haverton and the ladies?"

How was Catherine to tell the Duchess? Her son had attracted every female within eyesight—theirs not his. "I'm afraid that you may have underestimated his difficulties."

"Is that so? How interesting. Do go on."

"You see, I followed Lord Haverton to the garden. I thought he might have wanted to be alone but he hadn't asked me to remain behind. It was a bit awkward at first. I felt as if I were intruding on his privacy. It wasn't until a short while later that I understood why he had insisted I keep him in sight at all times."

"What happened?"

"At first, his lordship was alone. Then a young lady appeared, seemingly from nowhere. Thinking back on it, I suppose she must have been hiding there, waiting for him all along."

"Really?" The Duchess straightened in her seat.

"As it turns out the young lady was unchaperoned."

"Yes, I see." The Duchess hadn't envisioned that her

son was actually *prey*. If she had heard this tale from a man she might not have believed it. "Please continue."

"The young lady behaved very . . . well, her behavior was most . . . lacking what I would consider a proper lady's behavior." Catherine glanced from the Duchess back to her folded hands. "It was very awkward when I had to intervene. Lord Haverton praised my actions and assured me I behaved within complete accordance of my duties."

"And what was the reaction of the guests when they discovered you were Haverton's chaperone?"

"They thought it humorous at first. All of them laughed but then there were several gentlemen who exclaimed that it was a brilliant idea."

"Did they?" The Duchess touched a finger to her cheek in a very thoughtful manner. "Once we arrive at Madame Suchet's we shall hear the latest *on dit*. Let's not let on that you are Robert's chaperone. We'll keep our ears open and our lips sealed." Her Grace glanced out the window and patted Catherine on the arm. "Ah, here we are now."

Once inside, the Duchess made the introductions. She referred to Catherine as Miss Hayward and no more. No mention of her past, no mention of her connection to the Duchess and no mention of her current position.

Madame Suchet's maid brought tea. Catherine poured while the Duchess had private words with the seamstress.

"The other dresses can wait. The evening gowns cannot," Her Grace decreed, heading toward Catherine.

"She may choose from the collection of ready-made gowns," Madame Suchet replied. "There are several very fine gowns that, with some small alterations, can be ready in a day or two."

"She must have one by tomorrow evening. There can be no misunderstanding about that," the Duchess stated firmly.

"But of course. As you wish." Madame Suchet pulled out her tape and gestured for Catherine to stand on the box. The modiste hovered around Catherine, taking measurements and marking in a notepad.

In the momentary silence, the conversation from the next room drifted in.

"The Marquess of Haverton has hired a chaperone for himself!" a voice boomed from the room next door.

The Duchess sat positively motionless, holding her tea cup suspended in midair.

"It was astounding. I would not have believed it had I not seen it for myself," a second voice commented.

A red-faced Madame Suchet dashed to the door and latched it, much too late. "*Pardonez-moi*, I do not wish to cause you any embarrassment."

Catherine and the Duchess exchanged glances. At that moment, she had a peculiar feeling Her Grace was more concerned with what harm the gossip would do to Catherine than to her son.

"What's that they're saying about Lord Haverton?" the Duchess asked the modiste.

Madame Suchet's wide smile broke into a hardy

laugh. "I am sorry, Your Grace." She covered her mouth to staunch her outburst and took a moment before continuing. "It is the tale *fantastique*."

"Really?" Her Grace leaned forward with interest. "Oh, dear, and last night I had the bad fortune to attend a different affair. It seems I have missed all the excitement. Would you be so kind as to enlighten me?"

"It has been this way all morning. The patrons can talk of nothing else when they come in." Madame Suchet hesitated but after a few moments continued. "I believe half the Town's hopes are crushed. They say your son has hired a chaperone for himself."

"Really? That silly boy." The Duchess gasped as if this was the first she had heard of the amazing news. "What an astonishing story."

"It cannot be true. *C'est impossible*!"

"I cannot say what convention Haverton has chosen to dispense with this time. He is his own man, after all."

If Catherine had not known of her involvement herself, the Duchess' innocence would have sounded completely believable.

"And he paraded his chaperone in front of his gentlemen friends as he would a race horse," Madame Suchet announced.

Catherine gasped and met Her Grace's concerned gaze. It's not what happened at all but how was she to tell the Duchess that?

"I have also heard, from a reliable source, that he

has challenged all the ladies of England to try and ensnare him."

"That would be very foolish," the Duchess commented, feigning unconcern. "It certainly does not sound like my son."

"I have it on the best authority that he has taken his most daring flirting to the dance floor." Madame Suchet straightened and stared wide-eyed at Catherine. "Can you imagine? For all to see!"

And Catherine thought he was taking a break from picking up fans.

Madame Suchet finished her measurements and brought out the collection of ready-made gowns she had spoken of earlier. All the gowns were exquisite, spanning the colors of the rainbow. One was dark rose, the next a pale yellow, then a mild green, followed by a dark blue and finally a soft lavender. The Duchess pointed out those which she felt were appropriate, leaving the ultimate choice up to Catherine. She had a very hard time making up her mind until Her Grace announced that they would take them all.

"Have the green one ready for tomorrow night," she requested in a tone of authority.

Another hour was spent choosing styles from fashion plates and the next selecting appropriate fabrics for each style.

"I shall make sure the green gown is sent to Waverly Hall tomorrow afternoon."

"Excellent," the Duchess remarked.

In the privacy of the coach, Catherine finally asked, "I do not wish to be rude, Your Grace, but why did you have my gowns sent to your home?"

"Can you imagine the scandal that would have followed if Madame Suchet learned that you resided at Moreland Manor?"

"I'm afraid I had not." Catherine caught her lower lip between her teeth.

"The women of the Town are not known for their flattering praise. I think it might be best if we let your position remain a mystery for the time being, do you not agree?"

"I think that might be the thing to do." Catherine blinked. "I cannot believe everyone would be talking of such trivial matters."

"Trivial? You have no idea." The Duchess did not know how she could explain further and simply sighed. "My child, you do not understand the workings of the *ton*."

Chapter Five

Haverton awoke to a marvelous morning after the triumph at the Trowbridge soiree the previous evening. Last night had gone just as he had hoped. With his chaperone by his side, he felt he could enjoy the ball as a free man. He proceeded as he pleased, without worry of some woman hiding around every corner to waylay him.

A ride in the park would be just the thing to set the right tone for this day. There would be no need for Mrs. Hayes while he was out on horseback. He had never been accosted in the park before and did not expect to be bothered with only a few other gentlemen riders present.

He called for his bay hunter to be saddled while he took breakfast. A mere half hour later, he rode at a fast-paced trot and made good time to the park. Once he reached the path, he nudged his mount into an easy canter.

It hadn't been ten minutes before he heard several high-pitched calls for help. Haverton glanced behind him, trying to spot the source of the cries. The sound of thundering hoofbeats grew louder as the approaching gray runaway came up fast from behind. On its back was a woman in distress and clearly unable to gain control of her mount.

Haverton's bay surged forward. He checked the reins, held his horse from bolting and sat deep. The gray neared. The Marquess urged his horse forward to pursue and within seconds matched the gray's speed. Haverton stretched out his arm and reached for the rider. The woman grabbed for him and snatched him by the coat sleeve, successfully pulling him off his horse as she lost her seat, sending them both tumbling to the ground.

A few moments' silence ensued after their undignified landing. The Marquess sat up and craned his neck to check on the condition of the woman who had all but caused this disaster.

"Lord Haverton! Thank goodness it is you." It was Lady Darrow. Had he not seen her last night at the ball? Did he not dance with her daughter the lovely Miss Darrow?

"I do not believe it is such good fortune," he mumbled. Apparently the comment passed unheard. He stood and helped Lady Darrow to her feet before brushing the dust from his clothes.

"Please, . . ." she said in a soft, low tone, "allow me. It's the least I can do." Lady Darrow brushed the sleeve of his coat then she inched closer. He caught her arm by the wrist, preventing her from approaching areas she had no business near.

"I am fine." He noted that she had forgotten to feign helplessness and shock and seemed more interested in helping herself. All he could manage was a civil, "Are you harmed?"

Lady Darrow drew her wrist to her forehead and fluttered her eyelashes. Holding out her other arm, she gave an anguished sigh. "I suppose I am fine but . . . I feel . . . a trifle . . ." She wobbled a bit before swooning in just the right direction for Haverton to catch her.

What had probably hurt her the most was being found out, he mused. The Marquess laid Lady Darrow on the grass next to the bridal path and knelt by her side. His bay stood not ten feet away from him, grazing alongside Lady Darrow's gray.

He glanced down the path, looking, hoping, praying her riding companion would soon arrive. Anyone except her husband. Several minutes passed. No one was coming and Lady Darrow showed no signs of recovery. Would it be a terrible thing to leave her here? How wrong would it be to leap into his saddle and dash home? No, he couldn't do that, no matter how ill or premeditated her intent.

Haverton lowered himself to the grass and he sat. If she were unconscious, he was the King of England.

Resting his elbows on his knees, he concluded he was better off leaving her lie pretending unconsciousness than reviving her and having to fight her off.

Yes, he'd wait, but he would not enjoy it.

In the large parlor of Moreland Manor, Catherine discovered, to her delight, not a harpsichord but a pianoforte. The last time she had played was as a child while living at her grandfather's house. She sat on the bench and keyed a simple tune with her right hand. Her fingers were slow, proving that it had been too many years since she had last practiced.

Moving down an octave, she played the same tune with her left hand. Then again, down another octave. Instead of the plucked, tinny sound of the harpsichord, there was a wonderful low, sonorous vibration.

What a wonderful sounding instrument.

Catherine played a slow arpeggio, delighting in the tone and range. Out of the corner of her eye, she spotted someone hovering at the door and stopped, pulling her hands from the keyboard.

"Lord Simon, is it not?"

"Delighted to see you again, Mrs. Hayes." He came into the room and neared the piano. "I must relay my appreciation."

"In what way, my lord?"

"Because of your presence, you will, ultimately, give my brother the opportunity to choose his own wife. I suppose after he marries and provides an heir, I will be even more thankful that my name will remain Lord Simon and not a simple . . . Simon."

"Simple Simon?" Catherine bit her lips to keep from laughing.

Lord Simon chuckled. "It's only a jest." It was not long before Catherine joined him. Surely charm must run in the family for Simon was more than simple.

"Do you play?" He leaned against the piano, looking genuinely interested in what she had to say, quite unlike his brother. "I thought I heard *something* resembling music coming from this room."

Catherine started to move away from the instrument. "I'm sorry, I should not have assumed—"

"Nonsense, it's perfectly fine," Lord Simon said, motioning her to return to the seat. "Why should you not play? This instrument sits abandoned most of the time. The only other person who ever plays is me. Haverton has never shown any interest in music. He has other activities, I suppose, that take precedence."

Why had that come as a surprise? Because he had taken the time to learn? Or because she knew his brother had not?

Lord Simon pointed to the music drawer. "I say, have you found a piece for four hands there?"

"I cannot possibly accompany you . . . it's been years." Catherine slid from the chair.

"Well, Haverton's gone out riding. They expect him to be gone a good while longer."

The Marquess had ventured out of the house without

her? Catherine wondered if that had been wise then thought how silly it was to believe he could not remain safe outdoors in broad daylight.

"What shall we do while I wait for him?" Lord Simon scanned the room. He pointed at the game table with the chess pieces standing ready. "Do you play chess?"

Catherine followed Lord Simon to the waiting challenge. "I know *how* to play but as with my keyboard skills, I have not had much practice as of late."

"I propose it is time you brush up. We have at least an hour before my brother returns." Lord Simon positioned a chair on one side of the chess table for Catherine and pulled up another for himself. "Would you care to be white or black?"

Haverton had waited for a good forty minutes before someone arrived. All in all, he had weathered this crisis sustaining only minimal injury. He left the ungrateful Lady Darrow in Lord and Lady Lambourne's capable care. The Marquess then removed himself to White's for a much needed respite. The entire way there he scolded himself. It had been a mistake going out without his chaperone. How was it possible that he could not enjoy a simple ride in the park by himself?

At seeing the Marquess, Sir Giles shot to his feet. "Odd's fish, man! What the devil has happened to you?"

Haverton usually didn't give much thought to his appearance; James took care of that. The Marquess had left the house this morning with an intricately tied cravat and not a wrinkle in his forest-green riding jacket. He caught a glimpse of himself in a mirror. His crumpled cravat and his jacket's torn shoulder seams would have his valet tendering his resignation.

"Good Gad, Haverton, what have you been up to?" Brewster was the first to approach and offer a helpful hand, guiding him toward the group.

"I suppose you can say I've been playing hero." Haverton swiped at each sleeve. A small cloud of dust rose, causing him to cough.

"Here, you look as if you'll need this." Fitzgerald placed a glass in Haverton's hand. "Do tell us what adventure you've been up to."

"Thank you, Fitz." Haverton drank deep and managed to relax in the leather arm chair. "Can't seem to completely keep free of them."

"Some wretched female—who was she this time?" Brewster leaned forward, apparently as intrigued as Fitzgerald.

Haverton shook his head. He would not say.

"Was it Lady Amanda?" Sir Giles winked.

He shook his head again.

"Was it Miss Emma Worthington?" Fitzgerald asked.

"Gentlemen . . ." Haverton smiled. No matter what they said, he would not be persuaded. "Your friendship and your sympathy is all I require. I do not need to plunge anyone into scandal nor do I wish to encourage tongues to wag."

That was the last thing he wanted.

Lord Simon tipped his king in defeat. "There you are. You may think you do not play well but it seems you play well enough to trounce me."

"I am sorry." Catherine could not imagine how she had won.

"You must play Haverton. He might prove more of a challenge for you." Lord Simon busied himself by setting the chess pieces in their rightful places.

Catherine could not picture the Marquess sitting long enough to play a sedate game of chess. "I hardly think I shall have the opportunity to—" She turned to the hallway when she heard the male voices. "I believe his lordship has returned."

"And making a grand entrance in his own home I see." Lord Simon stood and headed toward the voices.

Catherine followed him to the foyer. They approached Lord Haverton from behind. It *was* Lord Haverton but something dreadful had happened to him. He sported a sizable scrape on his left cheekbone.

"Good Gad, Robert, who was she this time?" Lord Simon exclaimed without the briefest welcome.

Lord Haverton, who was clearly out of sorts, glared at his brother. "It appears I cannot step out of my own home without the protection of Mrs. Hayes."

That was a fairly backhanded compliment. Catherine

actually felt sympathy for him, and what came as a shock to her, protective. Her first instinct was to touch the injured cheek and check the swelling. Catherine reminded herself that she no longer looked over children. He did not require her to act as his nursemaid. She was certain his valet James could deal quite competently with the superficial injury.

It was a shame to mar the perfection of his beautiful face with that nasty scrape. What it did was give him a dashing, roguish quality. That's all Lord Haverton needed, something more to draw the ladies to his side.

Catherine smiled, feeling his allure strengthen. Then her heart warmed as she masked her newly uncovered emotions.

Oh, dear.

What a fuss females made over the scrape on Lord Haverton's cheek that night at the Sutherland rout. Believing he could make a safe journey from the front door to the ballroom, the Marquess had sent Mrs. Hayes ahead to wait for him in the ballroom. That proved to be a mistake.

Mrs. Lyndon-Smythe stopped him just inside the front door and soothed his cheek with a dab of her violet-scented silk handkerchief. She deemed it fortunate her daughter, the ever-lovely Camille, carried scented water with her at all times.

In the foyer Lady Stanhope called attention to the scrape on his cheek. The surrounding women closed in on him, proclaiming their own methods to augment the healing process. Managing to extricate himself from the women, he strode from the foyer, up the stairs to the doorway of the ballroom. Mrs. Hayes stood in the far corner. She nodded when she spotted his arrival and found herself a seat against the wall.

Haverton paused at the doorway straightening his sleeves. One would have thought he had been injured in battle and had come home to a hero's welcome.

The hostess, Mrs. Sutherland, caught up with him. "You must be in such pain," she remarked, her voice full of compassion. She called to a footman to bring the Marquess a chair.

"No, really, it's nothing." Not wanting to appear rude, he merely inched back out of her reach. "It's merely a scratch, that's all."

Lady Sutherland winced when she touched his face. "It is a *bad* scratch. I'm afraid I must ask you to refrain from dancing."

Was the hostess flirting with him? "I hardly think dancing can cause any further harm."

"What if you feel dizzy while on the dance floor?"

"I really doubt that—"

The chair arrived and she begged him to sit. "No, no, I must insist." She held up a hand, brooking no protest. "Doctor Sullivan shall arrive shortly and he will give a diagnosis."

Haverton had already refused James' treatment that

afternoon. He didn't need any type of medical aid, much less that of a doctor.

"He is my personal physician," Lady Sutherland announced. "Here"—she took him by the arm—"you must take care while we wait." A second chair arrived for the hostess to sit beside Haverton, effectively hoarding him until the doctor's arrival.

"My lady"—Haverton intended on voicing his displeasure—"I must assure you that I am in perfect health."

She scanned him from top to bottom, making him feel a bit uncomfortable with a penetrating gaze. "Please, my lord, please, I shall not have anyone say I have been neglectful of my guests."

Nothing he could say would make any difference. Haverton sat back and made himself comfortable.

"Allow me to examine your injury."

He wondered if 'no' would have been an acceptable answer. Probably not. He leaned forward, allowing the hostess to examine his cheek.

Approaching his minute abrasion, Lady Sutherland's face came within inches of his. Haverton had noticed small gasps and polite sighs from young misses in an attempt at flirtation but the same sounds coming from an elderly woman was another thing. Clearly Lady Sutherland was out of practice.

If Lady Sutherland wanted his adoration and attention, he would bestow it upon her. Haverton glanced at

her, into her eyes, and gave a low, deep moan. It proved
to be too much. A moment later, her eyes fluttered and
she fainted dead away. It was fortunate that her physician had, at that moment, happened to walk in.

Lord Haverton had not been as troublesome at this
party as he had been on their first outing. He spent a
great deal of time with the hostess for the majority of
the evening.

The new cotton green dress Catherine wore made her
feel uncomfortable. She thought this green too cheery,
too festive, too attractive, and thought she might be
calling undue attention to herself. However, looking
around at the guests, she had not observed anyone taking the slightest interest in her. No, even with a new
dress, no one bothered with her at all.

Someone bumped into her. "Oh, I beg your pardon!"
A woman holding an empty glass stepped back from
Catherine and stared, pointing at her skirts. "I am terri-
bly sorry. I've ruined your gown."

And so she had. Catherine held her skirts taut, displaying the deep red stain that started just under the high
waist and ran down to the hem. As much as she had not
wanted to be noticed, her new gown was the price she
paid for her invisibility.

"I am so sorry." The woman apologized again.

It was an accident, and Catherine did not wish to
leave her post. She glanced at her employer. He was still
occupied with the hostess. What was she to do? Cather-

ine could not remain there in her soiled gown nor did she feel right about abandoning Lord Haverton.

"You must rinse that wine out or it will ruin your dress," the woman fretted. "Let me help you."

It would take but a moment for Catherine to attend to her clothing. Surely she could leave him for a minute or two. "Yes, of course you're right."

"This way." The woman took Catherine by the arm and led her out of the ballroom and down the hall.

"Mrs. Hayes!" Lord Simon called to Catherine. She hid the stain from him in the folds of her gown. He smiled when she neared. "How lovely you—" His eyes widened when he detected something amiss. "What has happened?"

She did not know what to tell him. Her dress really didn't matter. More important, Catherine had left her post, and his brother stood unattended. "Lord Simon, I wonder if I might impose upon you?"

"I can see you are in distress. What is it I can do?"

Catherine could not, in good conscience, place her own needs above those of her employer. But did her appearance not reflect upon him? "I only wish a moment to wash out the stain. You see, I cannot leave Lord Haverton unattended."

"You're worried about my brother?" Lord Simon nearly choked on the words and replied with amusement, "Oh, I expect he'll manage."

"Manage what?" the Marquess said, startling Catherine from behind.

"Robert, Mrs. Hayes has had a mishap," Lord Simon explained. At his urging, she reluctantly allowed her employer to see the problem.

"I think it best we leave, then," Lord Haverton suggested after glancing down at her skirts.

"Yes, my lord." Catherine hated to ruin his evening but she wasn't about to disagree.

"Why don't you . . . do whatever you can now to clean your gown and I shall meet you at the carriage in a few minutes. I'll say my farewell to our hostess." With that, he strode away.

Giving Lady Sutherland his regrets at his early departure had taken less time than he imagined. Haverton bowed to the wisdom of his hostess in regards to his current injury. He went so far as to confess that she was correct regarding his well-being—he should have stayed home to recuperate. Her fervor and excitement that she had come to his aid was far too fatiguing for him. The Marquess could not have been happier for her valid and much welcomed excuse to flee. Perhaps he should give due credit to his chaperone.

There was no sign of Mrs. Hayes in the foyer and no trace of her on the front walk. His crested carriage pulled up in the drive and the footman opened the door. To his surprise, Mrs. Hayes had already boarded. He saw the dark hem of her gown pooled upon the floor. She sat in the corner, facing the back of the coach.

Haverton took the opposite seat and knocked on the roof, signaling the driver to depart.

He had left without her.

Lord Simon approached and cupped Catherine's elbow, guiding her to one side of the busy foyer of the Sutherland's house. "You seem to be in distress yet again, Mrs. Hayes."

How fortunate Lord Simon was here. When Catherine saw the Marquess enter his coach she'd assumed he would have waited for her but he had boarded and, a moment later, the coach drove off, leaving her stranded.

Her employer might have treated her with indifference but he had never been reckless or rude. Leaving her in the lurch would have been both.

"Mrs. Hayes?" Lord Simon repeated.

"Lord Haverton . . . he has left."

"Left? What do you mean left? Why would he—"

Catherine pointed out the door. "I saw his carriage leave, just now."

"Robert would never just leave you here." He paused. "Not intentionally, that is."

"Five minutes ago I would have agreed with you but I saw him with my own eyes. He . . . he boarded his carriage and left."

"There must be some mistake." Lord Simon looked as if he was trying to rationalize his brother's actions.

Yes, there had been a mistake. Catherine wondered if somehow she was the one who had made it.

Movement in the shadowed corner of the coach caught Haverton's attention. A moment later, Mrs. Hayes reached out a gloved hand for him.

"Mrs—" Haverton stopped when he recognized his traveling companion, not Mrs. Hayes, but Lady Andrew, wife of Lord Andrew Bowers.

"Come, Haverton," she purred, moving from her side of the transport to his. "Say you cannot refuse me."

Despite her most fervent wishes, he had to confess that he could and would very well do just that.

"I cannot wait any longer, Haverton." Lady Andrew pulled his face towards her. "I am yours for the taking!"

Haverton moved away from her and rapped for the driver. "The only place I'll take you is back to Sutherland's."

"Milord?" the driver called through the small door in the roof.

"Turn around. We are returning! Posthaste!"

"No!" she cried, making a last effort to draw him near.

Haverton held Lady Andrew at a distance. "I am afraid you have done yourself a disservice, madame. If you are seen leaving my carriage, your reputation may suffer."

"Or I may be envied," she replied with an elevated air.

Certainly having their names linked would cause her

no harm. After all, she was a married lady. "Think what you may but I shall lend no credence to your tale."

In the end, he opted for restricting her movement. It was all Haverton could do to remain out of her reach. There was nothing worse than a desperate woman.

Catherine felt desperate. It was more than being left behind. It was the matter of . . . well, she had lost her charge. What had happened to him?

"Do not fret, Mrs. Hayes, I shall see you safely home," Lord Simon assured her.

"I am not concerned for myself. It is Lord Haverton who may be in danger." Her employer might not have paid particular attention to her but she was certain he would not willingly have left without her.

"Haverton in danger?" Lord Simon reacted in a most comical fashion. He truly was a gentleman, showing the utmost concern for her and not for his brother.

"Perhaps not danger but he may fall into the wrong hands." Catherine had meant that literally—into a woman's deadly clutches. She hoped Lord Simon would not need any more of an explanation.

"I'm sure he is more than capable of taking care of himself."

Lord Simon simply did not understand the situation. Catherine's instinct told her something out of the ordinary had happened. "I know some woman has gone off with your brother. He must have been forced to leave."

"Forced? Do you mean against his will? Perhaps at gun point?" Lord Simon was on the verge of laughing out loud, which would have called further unwanted attention to their present circumstance.

He had not believed her, she feared, just as Catherine had not believed Lord Haverton when he first told her what women would do to gain his favor. Women *were* after him. Women who sometimes resorted to extreme measures to get what they wanted, namely him.

"Mrs. Hayes," Lord Simon called out from the window in the foyer, "Haverton's carriage has just pulled up."

Catherine ran to the window to see for herself. There was the Marquess' coach and moments later Lord Haverton stepped onto the front walk of the house.

Lord Simon remained at the window while Catherine moved to greet her employer at the front door.

"My word . . . Lady Andrew," Lord Simon managed to say between long pauses, clearly quite shocked.

The woman in the dark pelisse swept by them all and continued into the mansion.

Lord Simon looked at the Marquess, who did not let on that anything out of the ordinary had happened, and remarked, "Now that is a curious turn of events."

But what Catherine did not understand was why.

During the next week, Catherine traveled with the Marquess to and from every event. In her eyes, he proved to be the pattern card of propriety. Each evening he behaved as if she was part of the interior of the vehicle itself, as if she was an extra cushion upon the squabs.

Catherine felt safe enough while in his company. He had never looked twice at her. No, he had never even looked once. She was the employee and he the employer, their situation was as simple as that. Perhaps not so simple . . . she had to admit her admiration for him had grown as time went on. There really was no harm in that, was there?

They attended a ball, a fete, and a boat party. Her presence at these affairs was always unwelcome by certain mothers and married women but their reactions ranged from being blatantly ignored to being overtly outraged. Once she was asked to leave. Catherine refused to feel insulted, stood her ground and insisted she must stay—welcomed by them or not.

One afternoon in the drawing room of Moreland Manor, Catherine plied her needle and glanced at the Marquess as he read. It took absolutely no effort on his part to look so utterly handsome.

Catherine doubted there were many people who saw him in repose. The muscles of his face relaxed, his usual stiff, upright posture abandoned. He reclined on the sofa with his long legs stretched out, propped on the ottoman before him.

Hidden behind her needlework, she admired the way one side of his mouth pulled into an amused half-smile in reaction to what he read. It was adorable. It made her smile too. She did not know when the sentiment struck but sometime during that week the most unsettling feeling came over her.

She did not try to pinpoint when it happened but she was curious to know *what* it was about the Marquess that troubled her. Frustrated, Catherine stabbed the needle into her work and sighed.

The sound of a book hitting the floor with a thud seized Catherine's attention.

Lord Haverton glanced at her and murmured a mannerly, "I'm terrible sorry."

Her breath caught, realizing what it was that she found so disturbing. Catherine Hayward, chaperone to Robert Moreland, ninth Marquess of Haverton and future Duke of Waverly, was in love with her charge.

Chapter Six

What a horrid thing to admit. Catherine excused herself and dashed out of the room. At the end of the hallway, she fell back against the paneling and squeezed her eyes shut. Shock and confusion made the simple act of breathing difficult. Once the notion came to her, she could not share the room with him.

How could she have allowed this to happen? How long had she felt this way? Catherine hadn't the slightest idea. She only knew it was wrong. Nothing good could come of it.

She could no longer fault any ladies of London for falling in love with the Marquess. Did he not dance and flirt with them at parties? Display his impeccable charm and gallant behavior? He had done so much less with his chaperone, he simply sat there and read.

If Catherine could tumble headlong into the cream pot, what of them? She couldn't blame other women for tumbling alongside her. It seemed that Lord Haverton's mother had been correct. He was far too charming, far too handsome, and far too adored for his own good.

Catherine pressed her palms to her cheeks. They were warm. Thank heavens she had left the room. How would she explain the embarrassing flush of scarlet? And she could never, ever admit her true feelings to him.

It made no difference. She had to remember her place. She was his chaperone and that was all. One day she could look forward to being replaced by the woman he planned to marry and there would be no reason for Catherine to remain, but could she wait until that time came?

Breathing easier, she pushed off the paneling and continued in a lazy walk down the hall toward the rear gardens. What was the harm in indulging herself with thoughts of Haverton? Catherine smiled to herself and pivoted around, staring in his lordship's direction for a moment before heading down the hall once again.

Call it a silly fantasy, a wistful bit of imagination, but an illusion all the same. Her days were her own to daydream as she liked. She did not have to imagine attending a ball with the man of her dreams. Her evenings were already a string of parties with London's most desirable bachelor. Her smile widened.

She could enjoy herself in her harmless fantasies of the Marquess. Why not? She could delight in his charm, bathe in his beauty, and admire his physique all she liked.

For shame, she chided herself. What an immoral thought.

The moment the library door opened, Haverton jerked upright in his chair and slid the paper before him to one side.

"The Duchess of Waverly to see you, my lord." Maybury managed to jump out of the way before the Duchess ran him down.

"What are you working on there, Robert?" she demanded in quite an unpleasant tone, even for his mother.

"Nothing, just some correspondence." He retired his pencil and stood. "Have you come to see Mrs. Hayes?"

"*Mrs. Hayes?*" The Duchess grumbled, rounded the sofa, and took a seat. "Not this time. I've come to see you. Sit down next to me, if you please."

He moved with reluctance toward his mother and sat by her side. "We're not about to have that *talk* again, are we?" Haverton wasn't looking forward to this. He never had. Why must she put him through this at the beginning of each and every Season?

"Of course we are. I shall do my motherly duty and remind you of your family responsibility and you shall rebuff my attempt." She held up her hand to keep him from speaking. "I have not had my say yet, dear, and I shall not leave this house until you have given me a proper set down."

"Mother, must we go through this exercise?" Haverton was already exhausted before they began.

"We must. Now, listen to me, my lad, it's time you marry."

He groaned at her stubbornness. "I wish you wouldn't call me that. I have a title, a position. My name is Haverton."

"If I must refer to you by that, then you will refer to me as Your Grace." The Duchess stuck her nose into the air. "What a bunch of stuff and nonsense. Do not take that tone with me."

"I am a grown man. You talk to me as if I were nine years old."

"You're not nine now are you? You're three times that and it's about time you think about setting up your nursery."

"Should that not be my choice?" He knew it was his duty but he did not have to see to it today, or this year, or for the next several as far as he knew. What was the hurry?

"I'm sure your father would support me in this and point out that you have yet to take steps in that direction. You have not married nor have you a single prospect in mind."

"I assure you, Mother, that will not be a problem. When the time comes, I shall have my choice. I need not search and beg for any chit's hand."

"I know. You're such a beautiful boy." The smile she bestowed upon him was not a kind one.

"Mother"—he followed his mother's lead and stood when she rose—"I am *not* beautiful!"

Her Grace approached her son. She laid her hand upon his cheek and gave it an affectionate pat. "My dear boy, a mother always thinks of her children as beautiful." The Duchess crossed to the hearth. "Now let me see. You have always had eccentric tastes. Never doing the ordinary, that's always been you. Not many men could get away with what you do or how you treat society."

"I've had a very good teacher." He eyed his mother pointedly.

"You flatter me. And now back to your choice of bride . . . you must find her attractive, of course. We do not wish to encourage a roving eye."

He did not have a roving eye and he never would. When he chose a wife, Haverton expected to remain faithful.

"And you need not concern yourself with an heiress or marry for money. You've plenty of that."

Haverton hated to admit he and his mother could agree on something. But she was right, money would never need to play a part in his marriage.

"I think you should marry someone who also interests your mind."

His mother certainly had everything figured out. He intended to do just that. When the time was right. But until then he would need to tolerate her interference. First, there would be the list of young ladies she thought might show promise as the new marchioness.

The Duchess paced in front of the wide marble hearth. "Who have I seen this Season that might appeal to you? There is Sir Edward and Lady Dunstead's daughter. What is her name?" She turned toward him, hoping he might supply an answer. "Oh, yes, I believe it is Emma. I've heard she is simply a pure delight."

Emma Dunstead? If he recalled correctly, he had seen her at Brayburn's do. Had he not hid from her mother at the bottom of a garden pond? "This subject is not open for discussion."

"Then there is Mrs. Bartholomew's daughter, Constance." His mother turned and stepped in the opposite direction. "They've just returned from touring the continent. I understand Miss Bartholomew speaks five languages. Surely you must have one in common."

Was she so unacceptable she couldn't find a man in England to court her? Haverton doubted he'd be interested. "I refuse to dignify that statement with a response."

"What about the daughter of the Earl and Countess Darlington? Lady Honoria. I had heard you took some interest in her the other night."

Darlington? Honoria? The name didn't sound familiar. Perhaps he had danced with her, he couldn't recall specifically. "Mother, as I have said previously, I will not continue to speak on this matter. Now or at any other time. I do not understand why you feel it necessary to do so year after year."

"I suppose you are right." She sighed.

"I– I beg your pardon?" Just like that? She would end

her meddling into his personal affairs? Haverton thought that not likely to happen. It was more likely she would add to the list of his bride's qualifications next.

"We can agree you do not need to marry a fortune. You need not marry a lady for her beauty or position. However a suitable family background and good breeding will—"

"Mother, I don't need—"

"I quite understand." She was losing patience and her voice grew louder.

If she kept to the script she'd followed for the last four years, she'd now come to the part about how he needed to fulfill his duty to his heritage and ensure that the family line continues.

"If you would care to settle for someone with youth and looks you always could settle for someone like . . . your Mrs. Hayes, perhaps." And she wasn't laughing.

"My chaperone?" This discussion had taken a most odd turn.

"If it really doesn't matter to you whom you marry, then you need not look any further. She has everything you need."

"Mother, have you gone mad? Mrs. Hayes? You cannot be serious." Haverton huffed in disbelief. His mother did some very strange things on occasion but suggesting he marry his chaperone was about the most disturbing idea he had ever heard. "I do have my standards."

"I should hope so. At least I have gained your attention." His mother spoke stern and perhaps for the first time in years he really listened to her words. "Of course you cannot marry a chaperone. You need to consider your future bride's connections and pedigree. I would expect it does not include a simple country girl as a prospective wife for a future duke!"

Catherine stepped out of the house into the rear garden and drew in a deep, calming breath. She released it slowly. The afternoon air felt cool upon her burning cheeks. She had to get her mind away from thinking of him. Distract herself with other things she loved. The trees, the birds, the flowers.

The thought of the roses ahead drew her in their direction. Large buds covered the bushes and promised their fragrance in a few days when they would be in full bloom. Today the sweet scent of honeysuckle filled the air.

The soft crush of gravel caught her attention before she heard someone call out, "Mrs. Hayes!" Lord Simon strode purposefully toward her.

"Good afternoon to you, your lordship."

"I have come to see you and bring you this." He handed Catherine a packet of papers.

"Thank you very much." Catherine opened the packet and read the name on top of the score: "Moonlight Sonata" by Ludwig Van Beethoven. Lord Simon was very kind to think of her.

"The sentiment would be lacking if you did not return the favor by playing the piece for me."

He was doing the best he could to get her to play. "I cannot do this justice until I have properly practiced." It was the truth. Not only had she never set eyes on this piece, she had not had the pleasure of playing, not had the opportunity, for years.

"I quite understand. But I do expect to hear you play this for me some day. Is that fair?"

Catherine smiled. "Quite fair. I promise I shall practice. Will you play this for me now so I should know it?"

"All you need do is ask." He retrieved the sheet music and escorted Catherine inside to the music room. She stood by the piano while Simon set the music on the stand and played. And very masterfully, she thought.

"Very nice, Simon," the Duchess praised, entering the room. "Are you here to see your brother?"

"No, I've come to see Mrs. Hayes." Lord Simon stood and kissed his mother on the cheek.

"Yes, I see. *Mrs. Hayes*," she groaned. "I think you might do him a favor. He's in one of his difficult moods."

"It might not be the best time to speak to him at all, then." Lord Simon made a face, clearly not enthused at the thought of encountering the Marquess.

"Do cheer him up."

Simon stood. "I shall see what I can do. I make no promises."

"I can assure you, it will make life in general all that much easier to bear." Her Grace approached, nearing Catherine.

"This has been a decided pleasure, Mrs. Hayes, simply delightful. Shall we say until next time?" Before he left, Lord Simon stepped close to whisper, "Remember your promise to me."

"Yes, of course." Catherine smiled. "I shall not forget." She watched him leave then sat at the piano and fingered the first notes of "Moonlight Sonata." "I should feel very fortunate if I ever play as well as Lord Simon."

"You'll have more than enough time to catch up, I'll wager."

Catherine looked up, hopeful. "Do you think the Marquess would mind? My playing his pianoforte, that is?"

"He gave you run of the house, did he not? You may play if you wish."

Catherine blushed. "I would hate to presume."

"You presume nothing, *Miss Hayward*." Her Grace's mask of composure slid into place and she continued.

Miss Hayward, the Duchess had used her real name. It was the strangest feeling. Catherine's own name almost sounded odd and unfamiliar.

"Yes, *Miss Hayward* . . . So now my younger son is calling you Mrs. Hayes." She sighed and waved, excusing the futility of her trying to correct either of them. "There is nothing for it."

"I believe you are correct."

"I've come by this afternoon to drop off two more gowns for you."

"I do not know how to thank you, Your Grace."

The Duchess straightened, drawing herself to her full

stature. "Do not thank me, my dear. You forget it is Lord Haverton who is more than happy to foot the bill."

Haverton put down his pencil and pushed his work aside. Disturbed and agitated with his mother's annual address, he couldn't draw a straight line even if he put his mind to it.

Why the devil couldn't his mother leave well enough alone? The only thing worse than females chasing him was his mother pushing him toward the unruly crowd. Haverton wished to please her but he refused to marry simply because it was what she wished. If he had married the first time she had suggested it, this year would mark his fifth wedding anniversary.

He paced from the hearth to his desk and back again. This discussion became more disturbing as the years went on but he was not about to give in. No. He was not ready and nothing his mother said would make him change his mind.

"I just saw Mother on her way out." Simon had wandered into the library. "I have the most dreadful feeling I've missed something important."

That's all he needed, Simon to quiz him on Mother's lecture. "Mother wants me to marry." There was no need to say more.

"Did she mention anyone in particular this time?" Simon, who did not suffer the same fate as he, could not imagine how tiresome the exercise was.

"She did have several suggestions: Miss Constance

Bartholomew, Miss Emma Dunstead, and Lady Honoria Darlington."

"Lady Honoria?" There was a strange note in Simon's voice.

"Do you know her?"

Simon rubbed his chin. "Ah, yes. I do believe so."

Haverton would never mention their mother's outrageous suggestion that he consider Mrs. Hayes. It must have been his mother's idea of a joke. It wasn't at all funny. There was no reason for her to throw a servant at him because she was angry.

"Ah, now the Season has officially started. It doesn't truly start, you know, not until Mother states her list of eligibles. Is there something wrong with her suggestions?"

"No. I'm sure they are all young, charming, and very pretty," Haverton replied equitably.

"Do you object to marrying someone prettier than yourself?"

"I am *not* pretty!" His brother knew exactly what to say to anger him too.

Simon did his best to hide his nasty smile but he did not do it well. "If that is what you wish."

"I most certainly do." It was bad enough he had to live with his accursed visage, he did not need to be reminded. Twice within the same day, no less.

"I ran into Mrs. Hayes earlier."

"Did you?" Haverton rounded the end of his desk and seated himself.

"She's interested in music, more specifically, the pianoforte." Simon lifted a polished marble paperweight and studied its facets.

"Is she?" Not that it interested him in the least.

"Mrs. Hayes is a pure joy. I don't know why you'd waste your time at parties when you could be spending time with her. She can hold her own at chess and she's the most delightful wit. Didn't you know what a charming girl you've got under your own roof?"

Was Simon in collusion with their mother? Haverton wondered. His own brother acting against him? He rather thought not.

"How do you know so much about her?"

"We did more than play and discuss music, you know," Simon drawled in a suggestive tone.

Haverton schooled his face into an emotionless mask.

"I spoke with her. You learn all sorts of things when you converse with people."

"And what else have you learned?"

"Come now, you must know something of her?" Simon replaced the paperweight on the desk. "You should exchange words with her some time."

"Of course we've exchanged words." He had spoken to Mrs. Hayes on a daily basis, sometimes several times a day.

"Yes, of course you would have." Simon scratched his head. "Allow me to rephrase. Have you *listened* to anything she had to say?"

That gave Haverton pause. "As far as I can remember, she's never said a word to me."

"I don't doubt it. Not that you would have heard what she had to say if she had," Simon mumbled. "I don't think you notice half of what's going on around you."

Haverton looked up from his papers. "I'm sorry, Simon. Did you say something?"

Simon smiled and crossed his arms in front of his chest. "I believe that is the point exactly."

Settling into his coach across from his chaperone to leave for Lord Dibblee's that night, Haverton contemplated an eccentric thought.

Was Mrs. Hayes truly exceptional?

He drummed his fingers on his leg. He couldn't imagine. Could his chaperone outshine the other lovely ladies of London? He doubted that even more.

Just because he had been interested in young widows in the past did not mean he would involve himself with this one. Never in his life had he turned his eye onto a pretty servant girl.

However, he was curious. Haverton uncrossed his legs and straightened in his seat. Certainly, Mother was joking about him marrying Mrs. Hayes but whatever had Simon seen in her? Was she so very lovely? The Marquess decided that having a look at her for himself would not do any harm.

By the soft, flickering interior light of the carriage,

Haverton turned his head toward the corner where she sat and for the first time truly gazed upon his chaperone.

Catherine blinked and swallowed. She tried to swallow. Her mouth had gone dry. Lord Haverton had pulled the air from her lungs just as he had from the entire interior of the carriage, leaving her breathless.

He hadn't said a word. He just looked at her. Looked *at* her.

Was it her hair? Had a strand fallen from its place? Her new dress, perhaps? It was far from the diaphanous gowns many of the guests wore. Catherine's modest striped muslin gown was not as attractive as the green cotton she had worn, and ruined, last night. With the exception of her gowns, she hadn't changed her appearance since her arrival. Still, he studied her.

Time stretched on. He stared at her face, over her body, and into her eyes. And she couldn't help it. Catherine stared back.

He had dark eyes. Not black, but brown. She never knew eyes could be that brown. That penetrating. He wore a strange expression. Attraction? Curiosity? No, she'd describe it as interest.

The door opened, making her jump. She hadn't even felt the carriage stop. Catherine blinked again. The next thing she knew, she was entering the Dibblee residence. As usual, she followed the Marquess and he behaved as he usually did. He ignored her.

Catherine began to wonder if she had imagined it all. Had he really stared at her? Recalling the moments before her arrival caused heated blood to rush through her veins and caused her heart to beat a wild tattoo. She knew she had colored for her face burned.

To disappear among the dowagers and chaperones is all she wanted. Catherine strode to the far corner and sank onto a chair. His lordship would not stare at her here, in front of all these people, as he had in the carriage, would he?

No, he would not dare. Fumbling through her reticule, Catherine found her spectacles and pushed them onto her face. It was her bluestocking disguise that had never failed to make her feel unattractive and safe.

But Catherine could still feel it. His gaze upon her. She was certain. Rather than look at him, rather than meet his intriguing gaze, she would look elsewhere, anywhere.

But how could she? What a tangle. It would prove most difficult to watch over a charge whom one did not wish to see.

Chapter Seven

Haverton stood with Lord Fitzgerald in the ballroom but his mind was completely occupied with thoughts of his chaperone. From inside the carriage, he had had a very good look at Mrs. Hayes. Haverton did not find her to be an exceptional beauty nor was she the grand conversationalist Simon had purported her to be. She hadn't said a word during the entire journey.

"I say, Haverton, is that Sir Giles over there with his housekeeper?" Fitzgerald pointed across the room to the open double doors.

Haverton spotted Sir Giles and his . . . female companion. Was she his housekeeper? It was hard to say, definitely more domestic looking than genteel. Very hard to say indeed.

The couple approached and Sir Giles spoke first.

"Haverton, Fitzgerld, may I introduce my chaperone, Mrs. Davis." Mrs. Davis curtsied. "That will be all."

Mrs. Davis retreated, taking her place with the noticeably growing number of chaperones. It was quite clear their number had substantially increased.

"Haven't you moved up in the world," Fitzgerald voiced in a droll, uncompromising tone. "Wouldn't have thought you to have a problem with the ladies. You've the looks of a double-snouted boar."

"It's the well-endowed purse they're after," Sir Giles interjected, making himself sound worthy of employing a chaperone.

"From what I hear, that is the only thing you have to interest the ladies," Fitzgerald quipped.

"I say . . ." Sir Giles continued, ignoring Fitzgerald, directing his comments to Haverton. "If I can't make it work for me, what's the use of having it? Started looking for my own dragon the very next day."

"It pleases me that you've found contentment in the presence of a chaperone," Haverton added while not completely paying full attention to the conversation.

"Made a world of difference at Grafton's ball last night," Sir Giles added.

"I can agree with you there," Fitzgerald said. "Went to the Stoddard rout with Mrs. Fowler." He gestured to where she sat, in the chaperones' corner. "All went very well."

"Not you too, Fitz?" Haverton had hired his chaperone out of necessity. Had his friends followed his lead out of their convoluted idea of fashion?

Fitzgerald ignored the comment and whispered to Haverton. "Just look at that." Fitzgerald pointed across the room. "The chaperones far outnumber the dowagers—they nearly outnumber the guests."

"Don't be ridiculous, Fitz."

Fitzgerald chuckled in good humor. "If only they didn't look so dashed unpleasant."

"They have to look dog-faced, don't you know." Sir Giles joined the conversation. "Can't have a chaperone more lovely than the lady he courts."

"To be sure, the only one who could get away with it would be you, Haverton."

"What?" The Marquess had heard what Fitzgerald said but he hadn't quite understood why he had said it.

"Your chaperone, man," Fitzgerald clarified. "She is quite lovely. But only the real beauties are of interest to you."

"I hadn't noticed, really." Haverton lied. It had only been an hour earlier that he'd found that out for himself. Mrs. Hayes wasn't the middle-aged matron he'd originally thought. "Do you think so?"

"Simply fetching," Sir Giles agreed. "Well, old man, we're off to claim a partner for the next set. You?"

"No. I . . . I'm not . . ." Haverton couldn't help glancing toward the chaperone corner for another look at Mrs. Hayes. There must be something about her that drew high praise from those around him which he had overlooked.

Mrs. Hayes sat across the way, trying to blend into the wall, if he wasn't mistaken.

Was she hiding? From what? Or whom? He couldn't imagine.

'Fetching,' Sir Giles had said, which was only slightly different than his brother's opinion.

Was she really? It was hard to tell from this distance. What he needed was a closer look.

"Ah, there you are, Haverton." Brewster came striding toward him, halting his progress. "Are you or are you not going to sell me that bay?"

"I haven't made up my mind," Haverton replied, somewhat distracted.

"Haven't made up your mind?" Brewster glanced from Haverton's face to where he looked. "I see your difficulties."

"Difficulties?" The remark caught Haverton's attention. He didn't consider his chaperone a 'difficulty,' merely a curiosity. He turned his back and stepped farther away from Mrs. Hayes, hoping that would keep his mind on his present conversation.

However, Brewster kept looking in her direction. What disturbed the Marquess more was the approval in his acquaintance's eyes.

"The bay," Haverton said, trying to focus Brewster's attention back to the topic of horses.

"'Pon my word, can you see it?" Brewster's eyes were round as saucers.

"See what?"

"She's interested in you. Can see it in her eyes," Brewster announced like a man of the world. "And what a beauty she is."

"Are we speaking about the bay?"

"Oh, no. Something far more important than a horse. A woman."

Haverton turned to gaze at the woman Brewster spied. Mrs. Hayes gazed at him from across the room. Was Brewster mad, trying to make trouble? Was everyone plotting against him?

"That woman is my chaperone, not an eligible nor an appropriate choice for my attention." The suggestion made him angrier than he cared to admit.

"She's a woman, man. You may have your choice of the finest ladies but the rest of us mortals are not as fortunate."

"I'm afraid not." His friend would not foist Haverton's own chaperone on him—just as his mother had—not even in jest.

"I don't know what you're waiting for."

"It should make things very complicated." The Marquess would never consider dallying with one of his servants.

"Complicated? As it stands, you're the very devil to deal with now."

"What exactly do you mean by that?"

"You might ask yourself why you're keeping company by yourself these days. Haven't seen you at the club. Don't even want to sell me a horse." Brewster made his last comment regarding the bay and backed away from the Marquess.

Haverton wanted to be alone. He didn't need to hear his mother pushing him to marry. He didn't need to hear Simon singing praises of Mrs. Hayes nor his gentlemen friends joining in on the chorus.

He preferred his solitude. Solitude gave him time to think. Having his solitude presently meant he was not completely alone. Mrs. Hayes was merely a few moments away.

Glancing over his shoulder, he saw her watching him. His neckcloth seemed to be tightening around his neck, cutting off his air. He had to remove himself—away from the gaze of Mrs. Hayes.

He could no longer be in the same room with her. This was ridiculous, her presence had never affected him like this before. No female ever had this effect on him. Haverton glanced at her again then averted his eyes when she turned in his direction.

He squeezed his eyes closed, ran his finger under his collar and drew a ragged breath. The room was growing warmer by the moment and his collar was too tight. Mrs. Hayes observed his every move. He couldn't scratch his nose without her knowing which finger he used. Never was his urge to flee so strong. He needed to leave, remove himself from her view.

Haverton paused at the door and looked back. Mrs. Hayes was already moving toward him. Reason told him she was only performing her duty, following the instructions he had given her. Yet he couldn't escape the notion that he was being pursued, by his own chaperone no less.

The Marquess staggered toward the men's room. Stepping inside, he felt as if he had entered a sanctuary but glancing over his shoulder, the trailing Mrs. Hayes did not show any sign of slowing. Once he had stepped through the door, a liveried footman held up his hand and stopped her from entry.

"This is the men's room," the footman said. "No women allowed."

Her gaze darted about before she stepped away, backing into the long halfway.

"You'll have to wait elsewhere, miss," the footman instructed.

Haverton had hoped she would go back to the ballroom. What she did was find a seat in the hallway and sat to wait.

The Marquess paced from one side of the room to the other. If he stood near the wall next to the hearth, he could not see her. Nor could she see him. Crossing back in front of the door, Haverton couldn't stop himself from glancing at his chaperone seated outside the room.

Why did he insist on tormenting himself? This was madness. She held no interest for him, he told himself. He did *not* want her.

He would not, could not, allow such a thing to come to pass—to become involved with his chaperone was improper. The Marquess paced one way and then another, then back again at an increasing pace. Distracted by his own troubled thoughts, Haverton ran into a footman and fell to the floor unconscious.

Catherine had supervised the footmen loading her employer into his coach at the Dibblee residence. She was told that Lord Haverton's condition was due to a collision with a footman. Good Lord, how had he allowed that to happen? The servant seemed to have recovered but the Marquess had not. There was a sizeable lump on his right temple, just beyond the hairline. She would have thought he would awaken with all the jostling of the coach, but he remained unconscious during the entire journey home. Catherine grew concerned. Perhaps she would need to call for a physician.

Once they arrived at Moreland Manor, she expected Maybury would have retired for the evening. If she could just get the Marquess to his room his valet would then take over. And Catherine would be more than happy to turn his lordship over to James.

The carriage door opened and there were a few awkward moments when Catherine and the footman stared at one another in silence while she decided exactly how to manage.

"Would you help me see his lordship upstairs?" she asked the footman. Catherine pushed Lord Haverton upright, positioning him to exit.

The movement woke his lordship, who promptly ordered, "Yes, saddle my hunter, if you please. I'll be going out for a morning ride after I finish my morning tea." Which did not make any sense since it was the middle of the night and he was not dressed nor was he able to climb onto a mount—nor was he drinking tea. He had, after all, bumped his head and in doing so clearly must have addled his brain.

The footman took a good portion of the Marquess' weight but Catherine felt weighted down, making the ascent of the staircase difficult.

She was losing her grip. "He's slipping," she cried to the footman. "Stop for a moment, please." As requested, they paused and Catherine moved closer to Lord Haverton for a better hold. The solid feel of him pressed against her side and the intimate placement of her arm wrapped around his waist, holding him tight, weakened Catherine's knees. Would she be able to make it up the stairs?

He lifted his head and stared at Catherine through heavy-lidded eyes. "Telllll me, Mrs. Hayyyyes."

"What is it, my lord?" Catherine looked into his face, his very handsome, close face, and knew she shouldn't be this close, regardless of his condition.

"Did I"—he groaned—"enjoy"—he groaned again—"myself?" he asked with each step upward.

Between her current task and his proximity, Catherine was completely distracted and couldn't make out his query. "Did you what, my lord?" She never received an answer.

He moaned with every step they took up the staircase. He must be dreaming. In his current state, whatever could he find so pleasurable?

"You smell so sweet," he murmured with a smile.

Reaching the upper floor landing, they stopped a moment for Catherine to catch a much needed breath. Once at his bedchamber door, she leaned away from him, waiting for the footman to push the door open. "Let's place him on the bed," she instructed.

It was all the footman could do to get him on the bed. The Marquess didn't exactly fight them but Catherine found it difficult to pry his arms from her shoulders. If she hadn't known better, she would have thought Lord Haverton was working at cross purposes.

Catherine excused the footman with, "That will be all, thank you." She looked around for James. Where was the valet? Surely he must be here.

After a few minutes, she knew he wasn't coming. With James' absence, Catherine would have to see to Lord Haverton herself. It should not have been much different than seeing Tommy Talbot to bed.

Not much, she reminded herself.

Unprepared to touch his person, she started with his

shoes. His black pumps slipped off easily enough and she stood there wondering what do next. His stockings and silk breeches must remain. She refused to touch his lower limbs, which left her with the upper half of his body.

Catherine puzzled over how to remove his jacket. She rolled him from one side to the other before deciding it would not help. At this state of rest, Catherine thought it odd how heavy and hard his body was, unlike the limp, pliable Tommy Talbot.

She turned the Marquess onto his stomach and refused the temptation to set her foot on his back to remove each sleeve. With constant tugging, she coaxed the sleeves off and, finally, removed his coat, laying it, neatly folded, over a chair next to the bed. His bed.

She loosened and finally removed his cravat while sitting on the bed next to his shoulders. Setting the linen aside on the nightstand, Catherine pulled the collar of his shirt from his neck and he relaxed, nuzzling his cheek into her palm.

Catherine pulled her hand away. He looked so handsome—no, she amended, so beautiful—even in this state. Smoothing the front of his shirt with her hand, she felt the rise and fall of his breathing, and when she stilled her hand on his chest, the beating of his heart. Something told her he would be fine.

Pulling the counterpane under his arms and up to his chin, Catherine smiled, thinking her days of playing nursemaid were over. This was so much like tucking young Tommy in at night. She stopped in mid-reflex of bending down to give a good-night kiss on his forehead.

At the moment she bent down, Lord Haverton moved up. It seemed his lordship had an inordinate amount of strength when it came to drawing her toward him.

He brought her lips to his and he kissed her. Her heart sped, beating faster by the moment. She felt light-headed and if she couldn't break away soon, she'd lose all strength and collapse onto the bed. She could not struggle free, or was it she did not wish to?

Catherine could do nothing while he held tight. His hold relaxed and his head fell back onto the pillow. Breathless, she stepped back in surprise and shock that he had kissed her.

The silly man. Catherine touched her lips with her fingertips. How improper, how sinful, and how utterly delicious.

Haverton propped himself up on his elbows and winced at the bright morning light pouring through his bedroom window. He immediately thought better of opening his eyes and let his lids fall back into place. He wanted that confounded pounding to stop! His head throbbed.

After several more minutes, the Marquess managed to pry his eyes open. He was in his bed and in his own room. The hammering sound he thought was someone repairing the adjoining wall to his room was his pulse.

What the devil had happened to him? One minute he

was . . . some place and the next he was in his bed, nursing an aching head. Where had he been? The last thing he remembered was . . . was . . . he couldn't exactly recall.

A party, he was attending a party. Then he remembered his chaperone, Mrs. Hayes. He recalled seeing her face as she sat across the hall, just outside the door. Her ever-so-lovely face, peering in between the various guests passing between them and the footmen traversing the room with their trays.

Something, he did not know what, must have happened to him and he was brought home. Arriving at Moreland Manor, James would have seen him to bed. But the Marquess could not recall precisely what accounted for his loss of memory.

Haverton hated to think he might have done something improper in front of Mrs. Hayes. No matter. He'd make his apology to her. Regardless of what he had done. He'd explain that he could not remember.

The Marquess had dressed and carefully descended the stairs so as not to cause his head any further upset, only to endure someone playing the blasted pianoforte.

Haverton asked to be served coffee in his library and retreated behind its closed doors.

And still the music continued. The music, if one could call it music, consisted of three notes. Three repeated notes. Three notes that echoed up the stairwell, three notes that resonated down the main hall, the same three notes that sounded all through the bloody house.

Over, and over, and over, and again, and again, and . . . would it ever stop? Those three notes were driving him mad. He sat at his desk and clamped his hands over his ears, trying to keep their sound out of his head.

When was she going to go on with the rest of the piece? Play, Mrs. Hayes, for it was certainly Mrs. Hayes who sat at the pianoforte playing the same blasted three notes. That music might just be the end of him.

Silence. He did not know why, nor did he care, but the music stopped. Haverton drew in a deep breath, grateful for the reprieve, and leaned back in his chair. Now that quiet had returned he could think clearly once more and perhaps his head would begin to feel better. He managed to survive the morning and the next order of business was an apology to his chaperone.

Catherine couldn't concentrate on the music any longer. She thought if she strolled about the garden it would clear her head and help her get a hold of her rampant thoughts.

Last night's kiss. It was a horrible mistake. And she was quite certain the Marquess did not know what he was doing. What she truly wished was for him to slip his arms around her and hold her tightly against him, only this time she wished him awake.

For shame! She scolded herself silently.

It should have been wrong but she wanted more. Fulfilling her fantasy was definitely not in the best interest of her ward. She was supposed to protect him from women. She was to protect him from women, it seemed, like herself.

What was she going to do? She could not face Lord Haverton, knowing they had . . . always remembering their kiss. No, she thought. It would be best for both of them if she gave notice and found another position. Catherine stood on the back terrace, admiring the rear gardens.

"Mrs. Hayes!" Lord Haverton called to her from the house. He had never summoned her himself. He had always sent someone for her.

In a panic, Catherine moved toward him. "Is there something wrong? Are you feeling unwell? Is it your head?"

Lord Haverton descended the stone garden steps. He smiled. Smiled at her. His eyes held her captive while his expression made her feel positively light-headed and she forgot all the concerns that had plagued her just moments ago.

"I—" He was at a loss for words. Never before had she seen him as nervous or this awkward. "My head does not pain me . . . so much. Thank you."

"You hit it quite hard. I thought it might be a bit more serious than a bump. I was moments from calling for a physician."

His eyes widened and he moved to touch his injury. "I had no idea my condition was that serious. I thank you for your concern regarding my well-being." Clasping his hands behind his back, the Marquess moved off the stairs and joined her on the pebbled path. "Can you tell me . . . exactly what did I run into? A door? A wall? A stone pillar, perhaps?"

"A footman. He recovered well enough, but you bent his tray and broke six very fine crystal glasses. I believe there were a few gentlemen who lamented the loss of the spilt claret."

"I see." He behaved as if he had no memory of what transpired between them last night. "I am glad that there was minimal damage to all concerned."

"I believe the bump you sustained on your head was the worst of it."

"I can assure you that I have fully recovered." He drew in a deep breath then asked, "Would you care to take a turn in the garden?"

"Of course, my lord." And what else could she say? This was his house. She was in his employ and he had asked her to do nothing out of the ordinary. The Marquess wished to walk with her. The thought frightened her. It was worse than she could have imagined.

Catherine remembered she had used a similar ruse when getting to know the Talbot children when she had first arrived. She had asked the older boys Ethan and Tristian to show her some snails and had asked Charlotte which rose she thought was the most fragrant.

Asking their opinion had worked on the children to put them at ease with their new governess. However, she couldn't see the same tactic working on her. Catherine walked beside him, keeping to the right side of the pebbled path.

"How have you enjoyed your stay at Moreland Manor?" he asked, still sounding uncomfortable. "Are you finding everything to your liking?"

Lord Haverton made it sound as if she was a guest instead of an employee. "I have no complaints, my lord. I find Moreland Manor very agreeable."

"I have come to rely on your presence. I am finding social events more tolerable these days. I'm not quite sure if you know but before you came, I had the most horrendous time attending those things."

Catherine could well imagine. Lord Simon had told her stories of his brother's unfortunate situations. The image of a dripping wet Marquess emerging from a fountain came to mind.

"There is something else I wish to mention." He paused for a moment.

Catherine stopped and looked up at him. He squinted in the shaft of late afternoon sunlight falling through the tall trees. A warm breeze from the east swirled small leaves at their feet.

The time it took for him to continue felt like an eternity. Perhaps she had been wrong about his memory. Would he speak of their kiss? Would he, too, realize she could not continue in his employ and dismiss her?

"Do you like roses? We have a very fine display over there." He pointed off to his left.

"I must pay them particular attention on my next walk." Catherine motioned to her right. "I was admiring your honeysuckle just now. It is difficult for a rose or even a gardenia to match the sweet scent of common honeysuckle blossoms."

The Marquess glanced in the direction of the honeysuckle bush and inhaled. A momentary silence ensued before he shifted his attention back to her. "I have a confession to make. I must admit I do not recall leaving the party last night. I'm afraid I do not even recall the trip home. If I did or said anything . . . inappropriate, shall we say, I do most heartily apologize for my actions."

His confession shocked her.

He had no recollection whatsoever.

Because of their kiss, Catherine had doubts of whether she could continue to work for him. However, with Lord Haverton's inability to remember their indiscretion it would be possible for her to remain.

Yes, Catherine could continue. And she would never, ever admit to him that their kiss had happened. It would be her little secret.

Chapter Eight

Sitting in the theater box that night, Haverton felt the veritable fool when he finally remembered his fear regarding Mrs. Hayes watching him the night before at Dibblees'. Mrs. Hayes sat inconspicuously to his left, a row back. She was far more interested in the musical performances than she was in him, proving to Haverton that any notice she had taken in him had been imaginary.

This performance began with a violin virtuoso, Leonardo Benenati, who played to a full house. During the final interval the theater attendance grew for the much anticipated finale of the heralded Italian musician, Signore Giuseppe Genualdi, playing selected compositions of Herr Beethoven.

A footman entered the box and handed Haverton a slip of parchment. He unfolded the note.

Please come by and pay your respects. Celeste.

The Marquess looked from the note to the theater boxes across the way. Celeste was here, sitting four boxes to the left. And he would, as she had requested, pay his respects. He owed her that much. Their parting had been amicable, there was no reason to be uncivil now. He would gladly call on her as she asked.

Minutes later, Haverton stepped through the heavy drapes in Celeste's box. "Mrs. Cummings-Albright." He reached out to her.

Celeste closed her fingers over his hand and pulled him near. "Let's dispense with the formalities, shall we?" A sparkle glinted in her eyes and a half-smile transformed her lovely face into a warm and inviting one. "What a dear you are to come by to see me."

Haverton remembered just how inviting she could be. "How have you been, Celeste?"

"Not as well as if you kept my company," she whispered, leaning forward, pressing her jasmine-scented cheek to his. "But I see you have not been alone for long. Who is she?" Celeste tilted her head, indicating his box. More to the point, the solitary female occupying his box.

"The only woman in my life at the moment is my chaperone and she shouldn't cause anyone to be jealous."

"I am not jealous, pet. Just concerned," Celeste replied in a lilting coo. "You know how I worry about you."

Haverton's visit lasted only a few minutes. Long enough for a polite call and not long enough for him to get into trouble. Stepping into his own box, he remarked to his dutiful chaperone, "You see, I have returned quite safely."

Mrs. Hayes had been reluctant to let him venture out of her sight alone. He could see the amused look in her eyes when she smiled and nodded in return. The lights dimmed and the Marquess took his seat.

Grandmaster Signore Genualdi stepped onto the stage to thunderous applause. Adorned in evening attire with his long, dark hair bound at the back of his neck, he took a seat at the piano and began to play.

That's when Haverton's mind began to wander. Losing focus on the music, he wondered why he had bothered to attend at all. He had no interest in instrumental music. Why ever did he agree to attend?

The sight of Mrs. Hayes draping her arm over the chair in front of her for balance and staring through her opera glasses caught his attention. Her eyes widened in an expression of pure pleasure.

The answer came to him. It all seemed perfectly clear, then. This is why he had attended.

She loved music.

Commotion on the stage interrupted his reverie. The music continued with Signore Genualdi pounding on the piano with great force, á la Beethoven. Strands of his hair hung loose around his face, swaying to and fro as he played. But the commotion, it seemed, was caused by a second man who ran the length of the pianoforte and back again.

"What is that man doing down there?" Haverton remarked with new-found interest.

Mrs. Hayes leaned forward, looking closer through the opera glasses for an answer.

"Come sit here." He motioned for her to take the first row seat. "You'll be able to see much better."

At his suggestion, she took the seat in front of her and continued to watch the musician. "He is pulling the broken strings from the instrument," she whispered.

Signore Genualdi's assistant turned a page of music before running back to pull more broken strings. Did not the missing strings result in missing notes? Haverton wondered. Did it not matter to the piece of music he played?

Apparently not, no one complained. Everyone hung out of their box, mesmerized by the high drama taking place on the stage. At the end of the piece, Signore Genualdi sagged to one side, nearly falling off his seat in apparent exhaustion and uttered with his last breath, *"Non posso respirare."*

Every member of the audience gasped. Almost every member, except for Haverton, who smiled. With help from an off-stage hand, the page-turner carried the grand musician away.

Mrs. Hayes turned to the Marquess. "Do you think

he will be all right?" Her worried expression and tone showed her genuine concern. Apparently Signore Genualdi's performance had touched her.

"I think . . ." Haverton decided it might be better if he kept his double entendres to himself. He should not be flirting with his chaperone. "I should not worry, if I were you. I believe he will be just fine."

"Was he not wonderful?" she said quite freely, as if she was merely another patron of the arts in attendance.

"I have never seen the like of him before," Haverton replied with perfect honesty.

Signore Genualdi's assistant returned, stopping at center stage. He held his hands up to hush the crowd. *"Non si preoccupi!"* he announced. "Signore Genualdi will recover."

The applause and cheers of the audience rose with thanks of answered prayers. Mrs. Hayes eased back in her chair, smiling at Lord Haverton with relief.

"You see," he said, returning her smile, thinking her a silly thing but quite adorable for believing the staged finale. "Signore Genualdi will be fine."

The scent of roses filled the rear garden of Moreland Manor. It was a perfect afternoon that followed a perfect morning, and Catherine's life was about as perfect as it could be—barring any stray, occasional, or untoward thought regarding her employer, that is.

Lord Haverton kept to himself for the most part and her tender feelings for him did not matter. The evening in the carriage when he had stared at her seemed so long ago. Ages, in fact. She never had discovered what that was about.

Catherine strolled past the rose garden which was now in full bloom. A few, small sprouting weeds marred the rose bushes' perfection. She stepped close to the flower bed, bent to the ground to remove the intruders, then took another step, and another, and pulled a few more.

The sound of quick footfalls coming in her direction surprised Catherine. She straightened and instinctively moved away from the sound, causing her to step toward the rosebush. Her cry was followed by the sound of feet sliding in the gravel and another, more masculine, shout of astonishment from Lord Haverton.

"Goodness!" Catherine buried her earth-stained fingers in the folds of her skirt.

"What in heaven's name do you think you're doing, Mrs. Hayes?" He, too, stood abnormally straight with his arm behind his back. If she hadn't known better, she might have thought he was hiding something.

"I . . . I . . . I was just . . . ."

He looked at her with those dark, piercing eyes again. And again, every lucid thought flew out of her head. Lord Haverton stood wide-eyed, waiting for an explanation.

"I was just . . . there were weeds in the roses, you see—" She returned an equally awkward stare. Cather-

ine tried to move away from the rose bushes. "Oh, dear."
The hem of her dress caught on its thorns.

"Don't do that. Here, allow me to help you."

Just as the Marquess had bent and retrieved all those
fans at the Trowbridge ball, he knelt with the very same
patient gallantry, working her skirt free from the thorny
trap.

"There is a gardener to see to the care of the grounds,"
he told her, not in an unkind tone but scolding her all the
same, and continued to untangle the fabric. "You need
not bother dealing with the weeds."

"I was just walking by," she said in her defense and
shifted to her right. "There are only a few of them and
it's such a shame to have them ruin such a lovely
flower bed."

"You must stop moving away, Mrs. Hayes. Step
closer, you are tearing your skirts." Lord Haverton
circled his arm around both of her legs, drawing her
near, creating slack in the material. "You've managed
to make an excellent tangle out of your dress."

"My new dress," she lamented in a woeful tone.
Catherine's concern switched from her dress to Lord
Haverton. He held her very close and the Marquess'
touch was . . . was making her feel strange. No man had
ever touched her . . . there . . . on her lower limbs.

"Just give me a moment and I am sure I will be able
to set things to right." He knelt in the dirt and set to serious work.

She couldn't watch. Catherine could feel his arms encircling her legs but she didn't want to see him touching her. His nearness and intimacy made her feel less like a servant, very much like a woman.

Mrs. Hayes was all woman—soft, slender, a sweet-smelling put-together package. "Another step closer, if you will," he instructed around the paintbrush he held firm in his teeth. "I've almost managed to free you."

Maneuvering the twisted material, Haverton could not help but admire Mrs. Hayes' shapely calves and trim ankles. To gaze upon a lady's legs while under the pretense of aiding her shocked him.

"There." He cleared his throat and hid his paintbrush behind him again. "I believe that will do, with a minimum amount of damage."

Catherine ran her fingers over the punctured material and agreed. "Thank you, my lord." Her gaze moved past him to the end of the rose bed where she saw a canvas sitting on an easel.

"I'm afraid you've discovered my little secret," he said, not precisely ashamed.

"Your secret?" She glanced from him to the easel.

He hadn't wanted his fondness for unusual pastimes to be widely known. "One does not usually find gentlemen in the garden applying watercolors." He brought out the long-handled paintbrush from behind him.

"I see." The subject of the painting was the very flower bed that sat before them, surrounding a clump of yews. "I'm sorry to have disturbed you."

"I was having a hard time finding my muse this afternoon." She followed him as he stepped closer to the easel. He rinsed the brush in a jar of murky water. "I might as well give up the whole thing." The moment of inspiration was gone—well, redirected perhaps, he reluctantly admitted.

The soft crunch of footsteps on gravel announced another visitor. Mrs. Celeste Cummings-Albright approached the same rose bed where Mrs. Hayes had only minutes ago been tangled among the thorns.

"Haverton!" she called out with a smile and a wave.

"Celeste . . ." Her name died in his throat and he felt the paintbrush slip from his fingers.

As she approached them her smile stiffened. Celeste recoiled, brought her hand to her lips and looked from him to Mrs. Hayes and back again. "I'm afraid I've interrupted something."

Mrs. Hayes bent to retrieve the fallen object. "No, Lord Haverton was just admiring my work." She seated herself upon the stool and gestured to the easel with the end of the Marquess' paintbrush.

Stepping closer, Celeste regarded the half-completed work. "Yes, I see." She tilted her head this way and that, examining the painting. "Perhaps you will have time for a few more lessons," she suggested with a polite smile. "I think it might help."

"Thank you, I shall consider it," Mrs. Hayes said amicably and sent an uneasy glance the Marquess' way.

She's saved me yet again. Haverton was never more

grateful for Mrs. Hayes' presence and her ability to act swiftly. Perhaps his brother was correct and his chaperone deserved further consideration.

The Marquess held out his arm to Celeste and gestured away. "I believe Mrs. Hayes would appreciate it if we left her to her art."

Haverton did not want to give Celeste any reason to turn back toward Mrs. Hayes and led the way down the pebbled path. That was a sticky situation and Mrs. Hayes had handled it splendidly.

It had occurred to him that if Celeste had known that he was the true artist and not Mrs. Hayes, she would have pronounced the painting the greatest work of art since Rembrandt.

Celeste paused, tilting her head back just so, and peered over her shoulder at him. Even he could see how she affected a picturesque pose. Why did all of her actions seem planned?

"I really am sorry for intruding, Haverton."

"A visit from you is never an intrusion." He took her proffered hand and gently guided her along the path.

"How kind of you to say." Celeste's beautiful face positively glowed when she smiled. "However, my visit is not a social one."

"It isn't?" He felt relieved. He had thought she was trying to worm her way back into his life. This slightly improper visit would not be unexpected of her.

"I was out for a drive with Lord Fitzgerald and he was kind enough to stop here so I may return this." She held out a gold pocket watch in her palm. "I believe it is yours."

Haverton recognized the engraved gold case. "Yes, it is. Wherever did you find it?"

"On the floor of my theater box. It must have fallen when you stopped by."

"I'm sure it must have." Haverton couldn't imagine how he had managed to lose it but no harm done, his watch had been found. He took it from her and slipped it into his pocket. "I thank you for its return."

Celeste gave a satisfied sigh and announced, "Now that I've done my duty, I'd best be on my way. I am sure we shall cross paths before Season's end." She strolled back the way they had come. The path that would take her back to Mrs. Hayes.

The horrifying picture of a second encounter flashed into this mind. "Please!" He leaped forward, taking her by the arm, ensuring she would not go the wrong way. "Let me return you to Lord Fitzgerald. We'll take the long way."

Celeste smiled and lowered her lashes. "You must stop this, Haverton. You'll make me think you still care."

"You can stop painting now," Haverton announced, coming back from walking Celeste to her carriage. "She has gone."

With brush still in hand, Mrs. Hayes lowered her arm and relaxed. "I was afraid she'd return to give me some pointers. Who was that woman?"

"A lady of my acquaintance," he replied, not wanting to go into detail. It didn't matter, Celeste was his past and his future was . . . he looked at his chaperone . . . undecided.

"Oh, I see."

"Mrs. Cummings-Albright stopped by to return my pocket watch. It seems I dropped it along the way as I called on her last night."

"How kind of her to return it to you." Mrs. Hayes stepped away from the easel and handed the Marquess his paintbrush.

"Not as kind as you for accepting credit, such as it is, for my work. Apparently it is in need of further attention." He took hold of the brush as well as her gaze. "You saved me, you know. I could have faced possible social ridicule not to mention a harsh evaluation of my artistic abilities."

"It is my duty to protect you, is it not?" She relinquished her hold of the brush and turned away from him. "You were less than pleased that I discovered your hobby. I didn't think you'd want anyone else to know."

"And you were right. I jest about the social ridicule, although some of my unconventional ideas have been embraced. I think others would be less than kind if my painting were to become known."

"I do not think society would be as unforgiving as you believe. They seem to have accepted the idea of a man's chaperone well enough. Why should they not accept your chosen . . . pastime?"

"In this case, Mrs. Hayes, I feel they would look upon it as if I had a fondness for wearing ladies' undergarments."

She gasped. He recoiled. Mrs. Hayes was neither friend nor family that he should be talking so freely to her.

"I beg your pardon—I did not mean that I actually wear female undergarments—"

Mrs. Hayes gasped again.

"I don't—what I mean to say is—I should not have *said*—" He squeezed his eyes closed and tried to clear his head.

"I think it would be best if you said no more." She moved her hand to cover her expression but he caught a glimpse of her shy smile.

"I concur." He gave her a curt nod and returned to his easel.

"I believe I shall return to the house now."

Sharing these private moments with her made him wish for more private moments. Attending a party tonight would put her in an opposite corner of a ballroom. He didn't want that. He didn't want to make conversation with charming young misses and his bawdy chums, and he didn't want to share Mrs. Hayes with anyone.

"I thought we might stay in tonight," he called to her. She turned to face him. "That is, if you don't mind?"

"It is not for me to decide. Whatever your pleasure, your lordship," Mrs. Hayes replied in an amicable fashion then continued on her way.

Haverton held tight onto his softening heart. *If she only knew.*

Catherine glanced from her needlework to Lord Haverton, who sat across the room on the striped sofa, then to the flames in the hearth next to her.

Dinner had been tranquil that evening. Not that they usually conversed but tonight she sensed a different type of silence, an almost foreboding quiet that preceded a storm.

She wondered what he was thinking, or if he was thinking at all, and glanced at him again. He scribbled in a small ledger. His eyes narrowed, focused on the work in front of him.

Most people would have thought the Marquess busy, calculating estate figures or drafting an important letter. But the way his pencil moved in alternating slow and quick, long strokes, Catherine knew he was sketching. She stared down at her own work and smiled.

Only *she* would know that.

Lord Haverton broke the comfortable quiet. "Simon told me that you play chess." The long scratch of his pencil persisted in the background while he spoke.

"I play, my lord, but not well."

"I've heard you play well enough to best Simon." Haverton's hand stilled and he looked at her. "Could I interest you?"

Something told Catherine that engaging him in a

game would not be the wisest course of action but she could not refuse. "If you insist."

"It's not an order." A smile touched his lips. "I'm asking you. Would you care to play me a game?"

Just a game. Don't be silly, she scolded herself. What possible harm could it cause?

"Very well." Catherine set her embroidery aside and followed him to a table. He pulled out a box of chess pieces and set them on the board in their rightful places.

"White on the right, if I'm not mistaken," he said in a questioning tone.

Catherine nodded. How could he have forgotten? Simon said Lord Haverton was a most accomplished player. Why should she not play him a game? He had no ulterior motives—she knew better than that and she suspected he wouldn't attempt any childish pranks. For heaven's sakes, why was she worried? There was nothing to be lost for there would be no wager.

"I believe you have the first move," he pointed out, gesturing to his black men while she sat behind the rows of white.

Catherine moved her king's pawn forward. He copied her move.

She looked up at him. He smiled in return.

Catherine slid her king's bishop out four squares. Lord Haverton touched his king's bishop and glanced over at her, while he pondered, deliberating his next move.

The intensity of those eyes, his eyes, felt as if they pierced her, and all she could do was stare back. Her mouth parted, just a bit, attempting to draw a breath of air. But she couldn't. She couldn't move. All she could see were his eyes, his face.

Lord Haverton exhaled with a little sigh. Catherine blinked, recovering from her trance.

He cleared his throat. "I believe it's your turn."

Her turn? "Yes, I'm sorry." She had to stop meeting his gaze. Catherine dug in her pocket for her spectacles, slipped them on, and tried to interest herself in the chess game.

Again, she noted, he had mirrored her last move. Catherine could feel him looking at her, watching her. He was studying her face just as sure as he surveyed the chess game. Perhaps even more so. If he didn't switch tactics, she'd have his king in check in two moves.

Catherine pushed her queen diagonally to the furthest row and pushed her sliding spectacles back onto her face. She was hoping to find protection with them just as her queen defended her other chess pieces. But he kept looking at her with great interest.

Why did she feel so unprotected? She couldn't understand it, her dowdy disguise had never failed her before.

She looked absolutely ravishing in those spectacles. He'd never noticed until tonight. They added an air of mystery to her. Why didn't all women wear glasses?

Mrs. Hayes politely coughed behind her hand.

What? Oh, of course—his turn. Haverton stepped his king's pawn forward.

"Checkmate." Mrs. Hayes' queen sat diagonally from his king. "I do believe."

"I don't think I've ever been beaten that quickly."

"Perhaps your mind wasn't completely on the game," she suggested, keeping her eyes cast down. "Here, let me help you pick up," she added quickly. Catherine retrieved her pieces and moved to set them in their box.

Haverton caught her arm, stopping her mid-effort. "I'd like to pay my debt."

"There is no debt, my lord." Her puzzled expression made her look all the more adorable. "We did not wager on the game."

"But your victory must have a prize."

Lord Haverton made Catherine feel very strange. The butterfly she felt in her stomach before the game was joined by hundreds of others. The room began to feel very warm and her heart began to pound faster.

He moved toward her and gently removed her spectacles. "Why, Mrs. Hayes—you know, you are very beautiful." He ran a finger down the side of her cheek.

It felt wonderful and awful all at the same time. She knew Lord Haverton was using his well-honed skills on her. But why on her?

He made her feel as if she was the most important woman alive. He made her forget who she was, what she was doing, how she was supposed to behave. He made her believe the only thing that mattered was his touching her. And, oh, how she wanted him to touch her.

Catherine opened her eyes and held her breath. She felt the warmth of his hand move over her wrist and up her arm to pull her close. He paused at her neck and cradled her cheek in his palm.

Never in her life had she wanted to be kissed. She had never wanted a man to even touch her, that was . . . until now.

But this was not right. She should not allow this to happen, she thought at the last moment, but there was nothing she could do to prevent it. Lord Haverton inched toward her until she felt his lips press lightly, ever so gently to hers.

Catherine gave herself into the feeling of warmth and love and kissed him back. She nearly went limp in Lord Haverton's arms and her fingers relaxed, allowing the chess piece to slip from her fingers and tumble to the floor.

He pulled her close and whispered, "Mrs. Hayes . . ."

Catherine stiffened in his arms and pulled back, stepping back, away from him. "I am not *Mrs. Hayes*!" With a shake of her head she cleared the fog that had clouded her mind and realized the entirety of what had just occurred. "What have I done?" She had been caught up in some sort of madness. His madness. How could she have given herself to this unmindful, self-absorbed man? A man who did not even know her name.

"What?" he whispered. Her expression or behavior must have told him she was not accustomed to such intimacy.

"I can't believe I let you . . . let you . . ." She pressed her fingers to her lips, tears streaked down her face. "I am so ashamed."

"Please, Mrs. Hayes . . ." He laid a hand gently on her shoulder.

Catherine pulled away. She had to get away from him . . . away from here. "You—you don't even know my name—" She reached for the doorknob with her shaking hand.

"I know your name—" he offered weakly.

She opened the door and slammed it on her way out.

"It's . . . Catherine," he whispered into the empty room.

Chapter Nine

Why had she allowed him to kiss her? From the beginning, she had known caring for Lord Haverton was wrong. Why had she allowed herself to become attached to him? And she longed to know why he had encouraged her.

She'd never forget his smile, the warmth of his hands on her face and the way he looked at her. How wonderful it was. And how strange this kiss had varied from the last. This had been a soft, loving kiss.

Occupying the same room together would never be the same—could never be the same. For the last few hours, Catherine had reveled in her dreams, wishing there was a future for her and that man who told her she was beautiful.

But she had done the unthinkable and forgotten her

place and more important, who he was. She was a servant and would never be anything else.

A lesson hard learned and one Catherine would never forget.

His memory lapse had changed her mind about leaving after their first kiss but she knew they both carried a vivid memory of the second. She meant nothing to him. Catherine needed to distance her feelings and the only way to do that would be to distance herself. No longer would living under the same roof be possible. She had no other option but to leave. But she needed somewhere to go.

Perhaps the Duchess of Waverly, who had always shown her kindness, could find her another position. It was worth a try. Catherine sat at her writing desk and penned a note asking for an audience. As she wrote, questions plagued her.

Catherine ended the letter and signed her name. Her *real* name. Miss Catherine Hayward. She would send the note in the morning.

The Duchess of Waverly arrived at Moreland Manor the next morning to check on the status quo. Maybury trailed after her down the main hall, past the drawing room and the library. "I'm sorry, Your Grace, I have strict orders that his lordship not be disturbed."

The Duchess entered the breakfast room, still not believing Robert's absence. "Does that include his mother?"

The butler entered a few steps in the room. "I beg your pardon, Your Grace, but it does." The butler's bow displayed his deep regret at delivering the unpleasant news.

"I see. Very well, he is indisposed then." The Duchess scanned the room, taking in the feel of the manor. It was more than just the quiet hanging in the large rooms and long hallways of the house. There was an uneasy stillness in the air, evidence that something had happened.

Catherine Hayward stopped short when she entered the breakfast room. Her eyes widened and she gasped, the note she carried slipped from her fingertips.

"Your–Your Grace . . ." she managed to utter with apparent difficulty.

"Please come in, Miss Hayward. I was just about to sit and have a cup of coffee. Won't you keep me company?"

By this time Maybury had retrieved the wayward missive and held it out to its author, whose expression had changed from surprise to shock. The address faced up, clearly marked for all three to read: Duchess of Waverly, Waverly House.

"Is that meant for me?" The Duchess spoke first, breaking the awkward silence.

"No." Catherine snatched the letter from Maybury.

For an instant, Her Grace thought the young woman was about to cry. Oh, yes, something was very wrong.

She ordered the butler back to his post with a, "Leave us."

Once he left, Catherine could no longer contain her tears.

"Oh, my." The Duchess draped her arm around Catherine's shoulders and led her to the small sofa next to the window to comfort her. "Come here, dear. Please sit down. Let me get you something. Coffee? Tea?"

Staring down at her hands clasped in her lap, Catherine shook her head.

"Honesty, Miss Hayward. You know very well that I have always insisted we keep the truth between us." The Duchess pulled the letter free from its author and replaced it with a silk handkerchief. "There, there, you can confide in me. I know this must have something to do with my son . . . Robert. We women can talk to one another. The men just don't understand, do they? No, they cannot—"

"I allowed him to kiss me," Catherine said in a rush and looked up. "I must have done something to . . . to encourage him." She dried her eyes and wiped her nose. "I thought I was in love with him. I thought that . . . but I see now that it was not love. I . . . I . . ."

"A mother wants to think the best of her son. But even I must admit that my son is impulsive. He is prone to do whatever he wants and gives no thought to the consequence. You must not blame yourself. There are many young ladies who have given in to a moment's passion—and if anyone can create a moment's passion it is Haverton. I should have known this would happen."

The Duchess studied Catherine's melancholy face and sat quiet for a moment in guilty contemplation.

"In fact, I do not see what you could have done otherwise. You are very young and pretty. And Haverton is, well . . . I do not know a woman alive who could refuse him.

"It is my responsibility to remedy this situation, I know. You shall come with me and be my companion. Lord knows I need one. I come to Town all by myself. I shouldn't you know," she added, trying to cheer Catherine. "Now I shall have you. We'll get on fine, you'll see." The Duchess smiled, hoping to receive one in return. Or at least some sign of hope. "I insist, my dear."

"But what about my position here? The Marquess will need someone to—"

"Do not give another thought to his lordship. I shall deal with him." The Duchess gave Catherine's hand a squeeze, to give her strength. "You go and pack your things. We shall leave as soon as you're ready. Do not worry, Miss Hayward," she whispered, "I shall see to everything."

Haverton had spent the morning and almost the entire afternoon in his bedchamber. He did not want to be disturbed. After hours of soul searching, reprimanding himself, and general careful reconsideration of his chaperone, he knew that he should not have kissed her.

He hadn't seen her all day but that was his doing. Haverton had made sure he was unavailable to everyone. But now, now he wanted to—needed to see to her. She may not have been willingly to speak to him this morning any more than she was willing last night. But they could not ignore what had passed between them and they could not continue as they were.

Haverton dressed, went belowstairs. He was told she had left. The Marquess wanted to know where she had gone and when she would return. There was no answer given. A few minutes later he learned from Maybury that she hadn't just gone for the afternoon—Catherine, *Miss Hayward* had gone from Moreland Manor permanently.

He went to her rooms and found them empty. She had taken everything and gone to where? He did not know. The Marquess did not know where she had come from before she was here and had no idea where she might go to hide from him.

Sitting behind his desk in the library, Haverton ran his hand over his face in frustration. How could she, without a word to him, just leave? And what was he going to do about it?

Simon ambled into the room unannounced.

Haverton launched out of his chair and without a greeting he demanded, "Do you know where she's gone?"

"Who?" Simon was taken completely aback.

"Mrs. Hay—Miss Hayward, of course."

Simon arched an eyebrow. "*Miss Hayward* now, is it?"

"Apparently I was mistaken." Haverton sank into his chair, resigned to admit his error. "Had I an ounce of intelligence I would have remembered her entire name instead of the first syllable when we were introduced."

"Oh, I see. Well, I'm surprised you admit to as much." Simon teased. "In any case, you'll find her with Mother."

Haverton lifted his head and stared at his brother. "Where has Mother taken her?"

Taking his time, Simon sat and crossed his booted feet at the ankle, clearly delighted in knowing something his elder brother did not. "Hired her as a lady's companion, so I hear. Took her to Waverly House, I believe."

"But Miss Hayward is *my* chaperone." Haverton stood and jabbed at his chest with his finger. "She can't just leave—"

Maybury appeared at the door. "I'm sorry to disturb you, my lord, but there is a Mrs. Goddard to see your lordship."

Haverton looked from Simon to the butler. "What? I don't know any Mrs. . . . ."

"Goddard."

"Yes—well, whatever her name is, I do not know her."

"She has brought a letter of introduction from Her Grace, the Duchess of—"

"From Mother?" Haverton took the letter from Maybury. Glancing over the first few paragraphs, he saw no mention of Catherine or of her whereabouts, only an introduction of Mrs. Goddard as his new chaperone. New chaperone? He didn't want a new chaperone, he wanted Catherine back.

"Well, I suppose this does explain her presence. Show her into the front parlor. I shall be there momentarily."

"Yes, my lord." Maybury retreated.

Haverton sat on the edge of his desk. What was his mother up to now? Sending him a new chaperone and hiring away his old one from under him. All without his approval.

But he knew why she had done it. He knew exactly why. He had kissed Catherine.

Simon cleared his throat. "So? Who is this Mrs. Goddard?"

"It appears," Haverton began, none too pleased with the outlook of the day, "she is my new chaperone."

It seemed his mother saw to it that he was not inconvenienced when she removed Miss Hayward. Haverton glanced at Mrs. Goddard perched on the sofa. She might have worn spectacles and done up her brown hair in a bun like Catherine, but in no way was she similar.

Where Mrs. Goddard's bun made her look matronly, Catherine's was charming and her spectacles made her appear all the more adorable.

It was blatantly obvious that this time in choosing, the Duchess had chosen a woman with whom he would not be tempted.

Tempted? He was tempted all right. Tempted to see her to the front door. But he did have a vacant position and the amicability of Mrs. Goddard was neither here nor there. All that mattered was that she was qualified, and qualified she must be or his mother would not have sent her.

"Well, I see that my mother has explained the wages to you."

"Yes, my lord, she has told me everything."

Haverton hoped his mother had not told Mrs. Goddard *everything*.

"I have run of the house and most of the daytime hours off, unless you're in need of me." She looked him from bottom to top, which made him most uncomfortable.

"If that is all clear . . . as to your duties . . ." His concentration waned.

"Yes, my lord?" She stared at him with a look of adoration on her face that he had seen many times before.

"I wish . . . I wish for you to watch for unseemly behavior."

A blush washed up on her cheeks. "I'm sure, my lord, you have the exemplary manners of a gentleman. I've heard Her Grace say as much herself."

Haverton glanced up at Mrs. Goddard. "Not my behavior. It is the behavior of any lady in my company." As he said the words, they echoed in his mind. Were these not the exact ones he had said to Catherine on her first day? "Nothing suspect should transpire between any lady and myself. There should be no question of the propriety of our exchange."

Catherine . . .

Haverton had finished and left Mrs. Goddard sitting on the sofa.

"Shall we install her in the gold suite?" Maybury asked, catching Haverton coming out of the drawing room.

"No," came the immediate response. He would not tolerate the notion of someone else in Catherine's rooms. "Put her in the green suite."

The Marquess continued out of the house and toward the stables. If Catherine was at his mother's, then he'd go to Waverly Hall to see her.

He'd been riding a good half hour, another fifteen or twenty minutes and he'd be there. Haverton knew if he could speak to Catherine, just for a minute or two, he could convince her to return. He tethered his horse to a tall hedge off the main drive and traversed the remainder of the way to the east side of the house on foot.

During this time of the day, Catherine usually walked about the garden. He'd hoped that the well-manicured gardens of Waverly House might lure her outdoors.

Careful not to alert anyone to his presence, he made sure to tread lightly. The Marquess stepped over a small, trimmed hedge, rounding the corner to the back of the house. A window hinge screeched and female laughter drifted down from above. One of the maids had opened a window. Next he heard the sound of poured water—he was hoping it was water, for it covered him in an instant. More laughter.

Haverton gasped at the sudden drenching but remained silent. If he hadn't known better, he might have thought this had been done deliberately. However, that couldn't have been possible since no one knew he was there.

The cold water did nothing to deter him. He had to speak to Catherine. With the sweep of his hand, he pushed his dripping hair out of his eyes and wiped the water off his face before moving onward.

He took three more steps before he heard a second window open followed by giggling. The snap of a carpet, followed by a second, then a third being aired, sent dust and grit downward, clinging to his wet body. Haverton sputtered and coughed at the dust and dirt cascading around him. He couldn't address Catherine in this soiled state. She'd run the minute she laid eyes on him. He'd best wait for another time. After he had bathed and changed.

He backtracked to the east side of the house and lifted his foot to step over the low hedge.

"Robert!" his mother called from a ground floor window. "What do you think you are doing out there?"

He faced her, holding his drenched arms out to the side. "I . . . I've come to see . . . you, Mother."

"Well, stop lurking about and come in." She disappeared back into the house and shut the window.

The Duchess of Waverly watched Crawford hold the front door open. Robert carefully entered the house.

"What's happened to you?" The Duchess looked him over. Drenched but not to the point of soaking wet, Robert acted as if nothing had happened to him.

"I was just . . . I was admiring the ivy growing against the side of the house and the maids poured water out of the window. I suppose a few drops splattered onto me."

Splattered? The maids had splendid aim. They had hit their target completely. The dust and grit had added a special texture to his condition, just as if he had rolled about in the dirt like a pig.

"What is it you wish to see me about, dear?" The Duchess knew he wanted no such thing. He had come to see Catherine. She was too upset by half and prolonging Robert's agony would only do him good.

"I don't think I should sit on the furniture. As a matter of fact, I believe it best if I return home."

"I may be old but I'm not some half-witted female you can easily deceive. I know the reason why you're here. It's not me but Catherine you came to see. Why else would you be sneaking around." She had guessed correctly, Robert's dark expression confirmed that much. "I didn't think I raised a dolt for a son. You have done a grievous wrong. I am very disappointed in you."

"She's told you? I can't believe it."

"She didn't have to tell me—I saw it right away. You two have shared intimacies. Going back to you would be her decision, not mine. But I would not advise her to do so."

He pleaded with a damp, outstretched hand. "But Mother, I—"

"You cannot possibly be in love with her," the Duchess shouted, outraged at the very idea. "A simple country girl? A girl with no title, no position, no money? Doesn't that go against everything you believe in?"

Robert hung his head and exhaled.

"I thought not." The Duchess waved her son away. "Go back to flirting with your society ladies. Miss Hayward is not someone you can dally with. I can guarantee you, there will be consequences to pay if you come sniffing around her again."

Haverton's days were certainly dull without her. He tried going about his ordinary duties, pursuing his usual interests. But without her here . . . Catherine . . . there wasn't much joy in facing the day.

He never realized how one person could long for another's voice, laughter, and mere presence as much as he missed hers. The day could not begin without Catherine's warm smile in the morning. He sorely felt her absence across the breakfast table and having her ask in a whisper how his current painting was coming along. Not only had he not been able to concentrate on his art, it appeared he had misplaced his paint box. It normally rested on the table near his desk but after a thorough search it was not to be found.

"Are you looking for something, my lord?" Mrs. Goddard stepped into his study. She seemed to pop up at the most unexpected times.

"Well, I had thought there was a paint box here, some place."

"Oh, that. Left behind by your old chaperone, no doubt. I disposed of it."

He straightened, shocked by her reply. "You did what?"

"I didn't see the need to keep it around. I do not paint and you certainly have no use for it."

Haverton held back what would have been a very loud and harsh outburst. It wouldn't do to let out his secret, especially to this unfeeling dragon of a chaperone.

Catherine would have known and she would have never taken it upon herself to decide what to keep and what to discard.

"Just trying to be of service, your lordship."

"You've done quite enough already," he replied noncommittally. With that, she bowed and left.

Mrs. Gargoyle had thrown out his paints. Haverton sunk into his chair, opened his sketchbook, and flipped through the pages. He stopped when he came upon the sketch of Catherine he had done the night they played chess and had their first kiss. It made him smile.

It seemed so long ago. Ages, in fact.

The memory of her sharp, playful cry when the thorns on the rosebush snagged at her dress came back to him vividly. It was a delightful sound. He missed the lilt of her laughter which filled the evenings.

Catherine . . . Haverton couldn't stop thinking about her. Everything he did reminded him of her.

He remembered how she loved the piano and how she drove him half mad when she practiced Beethoven's "Moonlight Sonata." He chuckled.

How Haverton had cursed Simon for giving her that piece. How many times had he grimaced at those beginning notes? How he had wished she would stop her practicing. How he had wished never to hear that melody again. Now he'd give anything to hear those torturous notes.

He closed his eyes and focused. If he concentrated hard enough, he could almost hear her playing. There was a certain way the three rotating alto notes undulated as they floated down the hallway to his study. Then the lonely sounding soprano melody, chiming its way to—

Wait a minute, that wasn't his imagination. It was music—real music.

Catherine—she had come back!

The Marquess pushed away from his desk and ran down the long hall toward the drawing room. A million things rushed through his mind. What he would say, how he would apologize, how he'd beg her to stay. Whatever it took to keep her—

Haverton grasped the door frame of the large parlor and slid to a stop. Breathing hard, he stared at the musician sitting at the pianoforte.

Simon.

Simon lifted his fingers from the keyboard and glanced at his brother. "I never realized it before, Robert, but it's such a sad piece."

One chaperone was as good as another. That's what the Marquess kept telling himself as he readied for the Duke of Grafton's party. However, sitting across from Mrs. Goddard in the carriage wasn't half as pleasurable as sitting across from Catherine. He missed the stolen glances, the shy smiles that passed between them in the dimness of the transport.

Simon was right, he had to go on with his life the best he could. Haverton imagined that Catherine was doing the same, probably very merrily, without him. He hadn't planned on going out tonight. Earlier this evening he couldn't bear the thought of conversing with people or tolerating a party. The next moment, he couldn't face another evening at home alone, without her. He dressed and a scant half hour later Haverton was on his way to Grafton House.

Once inside he found his brother. "Is that your new chaperone? The same one?" Simon peered over and around the guests to catch a glimpse of her. "Heavens," he cried.

"Yes, that's Mrs. Goddard, Simon." Haverton glanced toward his new chaperone who seemed to fit in perfectly with the other chaperones and dowagers in their corner. The women dressed in modest gowns of subdued colors and wore lace caps. Catherine never could look a dowd, even in a drab-colored dress and severe bun.

"She's an evil-looking creature isn't she," Simon replied, not able to pull his gaze from the Medusa.

"Mother doesn't think I'll notice the difference."

"How could you not notice? You may be slightly oblivious, but you ain't blind, Robert."

"I am not oblivious. Mrs. Goddard—Mrs. Gargoyle suits her better."

Not only had she thrown away his paint box that afternoon, both Maybury and Mrs. Greenleigh complained about his chaperone ordering the staff about as if she was the mistress of the manor. That told him he wasn't the only person who might call her Mrs. Gargoyle behind her back. "One look at her and I'm put off my breakfast."

"She's hardly a gargoyle." Simon tilted his head for a different perspective. "Although one might call her a bit Friday-faced"—Simon turned back toward Haverton— "I am amazed you should notice though."

"Her looks have nothing to do with it—it's her manner." The truth of it was, she was not Catherine.

With this realization, Haverton began to doubt whether he would ever see Catherine again. His mother would see to that. What did he think he was doing here? Fleeing from his empty house wasn't the answer.

He had no intention of pasting on a smile and feigning politeness. He did not wish to put up with London society—kiss ladies' hands and dance the night away. He wanted to go home.

Escaping the ballroom in search of a footman to call for his carriage, Haverton heard his mother's voice from the front door, and then a softer voice. He was certain that it belonged to Catherine . . . or was it merely wishful thinking on his part?

The Marquess backed to a wall and peered into the foyer. His pulse raced. He hardly knew what to do. This was his chance, but how was he to see her alone? How would he—then out stepped his mother.

"I'll meet you in the ballroom, my dear. I'm just going to have a word with our hostess."

Haverton stepped behind a marble column and moved, keeping his mother on the opposite side, keeping him from her line of sight. Which left him alone with Catherine, if only for a moment. A moment would be all he needed.

He waited for her to step into the hallway, where they would be away from the blue and gold liveried footmen attending the door.

Haverton waited. His heart pounded so hard he

thought it would leap out of his chest. Feeling the dampness of his palms despite his gloves, he rubbed his hands together in anticipation.

A minute more. A few more seconds.

Catherine stepped into the hallway, and he took an unsteady step toward her.

"Catherine?"

Chapter Ten

Lady Darlington hid behind a pillar, suspecting something havey-cavey going on when she spied Lord Haverton doing the same.

The woman he called *Catherine* gasped and clutched her throat, surprised by the Marquess' summons. "What do you want?"

"I only want a moment—a chance to speak to you." He reached out for her with a slow and deliberate movement and took her by the hand. She pulled back, clearly wanting no part of him. Yet she said nothing more. He held her hand firm but not in a threatening manner.

Lady Darlington looked from Haverton to Catherine. There was definitely something peculiar about the way he stared at her and the way she returned his gaze. Something in their manner implied forbidden love. But the Marquess? How could that be?

"Please, just a few minutes," he pleaded. Never had Lady Darlington heard such a tone from the Marquess of Haverton. He had always been authoritative and commanding in every situation. She could never imagine him begging any woman.

"No, I can't . . . I shouldn't"—Catherine glanced toward the ballroom—"Her Grace is waiting for me."

"She won't mind a brief delay. I must speak to you."

"No. There is nothing more to say and . . . please . . . I must leave." Again she attempted to pull free.

"As you wish." He released her hand and she left without a look back. Taking a long drawn breath, he slumped back against a column and remained there for a few minutes before returning to the ballroom.

What had happened? Lady Darlington wondered who was this *Catherine* to refuse Lord Haverton. Then an idea came to her.

Pulling Honoria from the ballroom as tactfully as possible, Lady Darlington rushed her daughter into a small room and began plucking the bows from the shoulders of her new gown.

"My dress! My dress!" Honoria cried but did not stop her mother.

"Your gown is white but I don't think it will matter," Lady Darlington decided, remembering Catherine's as light peach. Lifting the hem, she tore off the silk ribbons, simplifying the silhouette so that she should appear more like Catherine.

Haverton would not come to Honoria but he would come to Catherine. Surely *Catherine* could be played by her own daughter. Therefore Honoria would be transformed into Catherine.

"Mama, what are you doing?" Honoria stood motionless.

Lady Darlington sat at a desk, quickly penned a note, and handed it to a footman for delivery.

"Come with me." Lady Darlington headed toward the side gardens, pulling her daughter behind her the entire way.

"You won't ruin our chance with Haverton this time."

"Lord Haverton, again?" she whined. "But Mama, he frightens me."

"Nonsense." Lady Darlington gave Honoria's shoulders a shake, straightening her posture, and hopefully jarring some sense into her dim-witted daughter. "This time you will remain silent. Not a word. Do you understand me? Do not say a word, do not do anything."

Honoria nodded.

"That's right." This time her plan would work, Lady Darlington vowed. She planted Honoria in the perfect spot, where the Marquess would see her yet not see who she was.

A few last-minute instructions: "Stay out of the light. Don't let him see your face. And above all, do not be a simpering miss but a woman."

Lady Darlington stepped into the shadows out of sight. She would wait until they were in each others' arms and then she would have him.

After ordering his new chaperone to remain in the ballroom, Haverton stepped into the side garden, the place where Catherine had agreed to meet him after a change of heart. He promised himself to mind his manners and keep his hands to himself. He had to convince her to return to Moreland Manor.

Folding and refolding her note in his hands, Haverton waited for Catherine's arrival as patiently as he could manage. This was the opportunity he'd been waiting for. Yet when he thought of what he should say, words failed him.

I'm sorry. Had I realized—I hadn't meant to— No . . . nothing seemed appropriate.

The sound of soft footsteps distracted him. He caught the slight movement in the shadows. She was here.

Haverton cleared his throat. His stomach felt most unwell but he had to continue. "I cannot thank you enough for reconsidering . . ." he whispered to her.

She held her arms out wide. An invitation? He ought not but he couldn't find the strength to refuse. Stepping closer, he slipped his arms around her.

At the same moment he drew her near, he knew this woman was not Catherine. His arms didn't fit around her the same, the scent of her hair and skin were different. He made to move back, away from her.

She cried out, "I cannot do this!" tore out of his arms and ran from the garden.

It had all happened so quickly but clearly he had been mistaken. He hadn't time to pose any questions before a second figure appeared. She had arrived. Catherine. For surely this time it was her. "Is it really you?"

She nodded.

He may have well been suspicious as the first young lady went away screeching. Enough to alarm anyone, even the Marquess.

He pointed across the garden. "I'm sorry if you saw that. I thought she was you."

The sight of her outstretched arms beckoned him near. She approached him intent on kissing him. He realized that this woman was not Catherine either.

Haverton made to move away from her. "No, you're not her."

"No, but I can be anyone you want me to be."

"Celeste!" Haverton stepped back, breaking contact at the sound of her voice.

"I'm sorry, *cher*." She smiled. "Seeing you out here alone . . . I simply could not resist."

Gazing out the window of the ballroom, Catherine had found him. Them . . . together . . . standing in the garden. Lord Haverton and his *acquaintance* Mrs. Cummings-Albright. To Catherine she looked much more than just a casual acquaintance.

He faced Catherine with Mrs. Cummings-Albright

between them. Catherine saw Lord Haverton's every expression clearly. His attention was focused on the beautiful woman in his arms. He pulled her into his arms. The look in his eyes was soft but intense, the same way he had looked at Catherine before he had kissed her. She couldn't watch anymore.

Catherine felt tears beginning and turned away.

Haverton had caught Catherine's reaction the moment he had taken Celeste into his arms. Catherine's wounded expression and the pain in her eyes mirrored his own discomfort when he realized the mistake he had made—but it was too late. He'd glimpsed her standing at the window and when he looked back, she had gone.

"No," he continued, moving away from Celeste. "This is what neither of us wants." Last year he courted her and she had wanted to marry. He hadn't been interested in taking that step with her.

Celeste smoothed her dress, readying herself to rejoin the other guests. "I see we may have gotten a little ahead of ourselves." She smiled and caressed his cheek. "We are caught up in our old habits."

"I suppose," he murmured. The last thing he was going to do was tell her the truth.

"Now that we've had our folly, shall we rejoin the others?" Celeste left him for the ballroom.

Folly she called it. Who knows what Catherine thought? Haverton stared back at the window. He would never forget the pain in her eyes. And he would never forget that he was the one who put it there.

An unfeeling cad, that's what he was.

Despicable.

Unacceptable.

He wouldn't blame her if she never spoke to him again. It's not what he wanted but he would completely understand. By the time he had returned to the ballroom, Haverton had puzzled out that the note had been a ruse. He didn't care about the who and why of it right now. All that mattered was Catherine hadn't written the note. She had never been involved.

And with this revelation, he wanted to, more than ever, see her again. "Where is Mother, Simon?"

"Mother and Miss Hayward have left for the evening."

"Left?" Then it was too late. He would have to come up with another way to see her. Alone.

Draped over the leather winged-backed chairs some two hours later in the study of Moreland Manor, Haverton and Simon gazed into the fire.

"If a man were truly in love with a woman, he should tell her. He shouldn't keep it locked up inside." Simon thumped on his chest with his fist. "What if she never knows?"

How had Simon known exactly what to say? Somehow he had known precisely what Haverton was feeling. "It's not that a man shouldn't ignore a woman if he finds her agreeable . . . it's not right . . ." Haverton added to Simon's discourse. "He might . . . she might . . . sometimes they cannot . . ."

"One can't alter social conventions." Simon shrugged. "It's just not done . . . surely anyone can understand that."

Haverton nodded. "You're quite right, anyone should understand that propriety must be maintained."

"But it doesn't make the ache any easier to tolerate." Simon laid his hand over his heart.

"No, it doesn't." Haverton turned his head, looking away from the fire, and regarded his brother. "What am I to do, then?"

Simon faced the Marquess. "You? What do you mean you? Who are you talking about?"

"Why, Catherine, of course, who else?"

"Catherine?" Simon narrowed his eyes. "I thought you were . . . what I mean to say is . . . I—" He cleared his throat. "Catherine . . . Miss Hayward, I thought you were merely . . . of course we're talking about Catherine. Do you love her, then?"

"Love?" Haverton stared back into the fire. It didn't hold the answer. "I hardly think I would go that far."

"From what I hear you can't manage another single day without her." Simon's voice sounded calm, reasonable, and sympathetic.

"Did I say that?" Haverton hadn't remembered uttering those precise words but that was what he had been thinking.

"That's what I heard."

"I don't believe . . . well, one ought to think . . . dash it, Simon, I do not know." Haverton rubbed his eyes and aching forehead. He hadn't been sleeping well and he hadn't been able to think clearly or concentrate.

Someone cleared their throat, politely interrupting the brothers.

"What is it, Maybury?"

"This has just been delivered, my lord."

Haverton gestured for his butler to advance. Maybury stepped forward and bent toward Simon, proffering a missive on a silver salver.

Simon straightened in shock. "For me?"

"Yes, my lord." Maybury retreated.

"Who is it from?" Haverton asked.

"Mother."

"Mother? What a relief." It seemed this evening was full of surprises. A summons from his mother would be the topper to one of the worst days in his life.

"A relief? Do you realize a summons at this time of night could be disastrous?" Simon worked the parchment open.

"Exactly. The message is addressed to you not me." Haverton was very thankful.

"Aren't you the slightest bit interested in what she's up to?" He began to read. "You must know that there's always something—" Reaching the end, Simon folded the letter and tapped it in his palm then stood to leave. "I'd best be off to see her then."

After Simon left, it occurred to Haverton that if Simon was busy with their mother, that would leave Catherine alone. He straightened in his chair.

If he were to . . . no, he couldn't do that.

Haverton stood. But it would be the only place where he knew he would see her. She had to sleep sometime, and if he was waiting in her room, she would have to talk to him.

He strode to his desk. Was he in love with Catherine? He hadn't really thought about it before Simon had posed the question.

All he knew was that he didn't just want Catherine back as his chaperone. He wanted her back under his roof, he wanted to hold her in his arms. He wanted to see her smile, hear her voice, and her laughter. He admitted to himself during his final deliberation that if the complete truth be known, he would have to confess that he wanted her with him forever.

Simon had been correct. Haverton did not want to live another day without Catherine in his life. If it meant marriage, then wed her he would, despite his mother's protests. He had no doubt he would need to go to battle with his mother to marry the woman he loved. This is what he wanted more than anything, but first he needed to convince Catherine.

The Duchess of Waverly answered the knock at the front door of Waverly Hall.

"Mother?" Simon stepped inside and closed the door. "Where's Crawford?"

"I've given him the night off." The Duchess offered her cheek to her son.

He kissed her. "What about Mrs. Lange?"

"Her, too. The whole staff is gone." The Duchess headed for the small parlor in the rear of the house. "I've given them all the night off and paid for their way to Vauxhall Gardens."

"What on earth for?" Simon asked, trailing his mother.

"I wanted the house to be empty."

Simon stopped in the hallway. "Then why am I here?"

"You didn't say a word to your brother did you?" She sat in her chair next to the hearth.

Simon strolled into the room and leaned against the mantle, resting his booted foot on the fender. "Well, he was right there when I received your summons. Normally he'd want to know the details but he was so distracted."

"Distracted, was he?" The Duchess smiled.

"I've never seen him so out of sorts."

"Good."

"Good?" Simon glared at her as if she should have had more *motherly* concern about her eldest. "Mother . . . Robert was dithering."

"Dithering, was he? Even better."

"You know, Mother, sometimes I really do not understand you."

The Duchess pointed to the seat across from her. "Come sit over here and give your poor, feeble mother a hand."

"You are neither poor nor feeble." Simon sat anyway.

The Duchess motioned for him to hold up his hands and she dropped a loop of yarn over them. She took the end and began to wind a ball.

He regarded the yarn then his mother. "Isn't this why you've hired Mrs. Hay—I beg your pardon—Miss Hayward?"

Simon knew Catherine's true name. *That he learned from his older brother*. Without cracking a smile, she replied, "Miss Hayward has retired for the evening. I'm afraid she has quite enough to deal with at present."

A loud thump from above drew Simon's attention. He stared toward the ceiling. "I thought you said the staff was out."

"They are." The ball of yarn was now the size of a plum.

A second and third thump sounded. Simon stared at the ceiling again. "What the devil is that, then?"

Her hands stilled and she tilted her head ever-so-slightly back, listening carefully. "I imagine that's the sound of your brother's standards dropping."

"Robert is here?" Simon launched out of the chair, gawking at his mother.

"Please sit down. You are making this exceedingly difficult." She drew back her outstretched arms to her sides as Simon, once again, sat in his chair.

"What is Robert doing here?"

"Attending to Catherine unless I am mistaken."

"He's with Miss Hayward?" Simon took to his feet again.

"Please, Simon, be seated." The Duchess motioned for him to return to his chair. "We need to wait just a bit longer."

After several minutes, and more than a few anxious glances from Simon, she finished winding her ball of yarn, set it in her basket, and said, "Let's see what they are up to, shall we?"

Upstairs, tucked in her bed, Catherine lifted her head when she heard the sound of something rattling or knocking against the house, just outside her bedroom. When the window flew open, she jolted upright, sitting straight up in bed.

Two large hands shot through the window and gripped the frame. He—for it was a he, she realized—worked at pulling himself the rest of the way through the opening.

Catherine wanted to run to the door—to escape—but couldn't move. She tried to scream but her throat was too tight with fear for anything more than a strangled sound to emerge.

He stepped into her room with one foot and apparently had trouble with the other. The toe of his boot caught on the sill and he deposited himself with an echoing thud onto her bedroom floor.

"Bloody hell," came the partially suppressed oath.

Catherine knew that voice. And she realized there was something familiar about the silhouetted form, before he fell. The shadowed shape of the head, the arch of his back, the way his arms moved as he came through the window. If she was not mistaken, she would have thought it was . . . he was . . .

"Lord Haverton?" He had come. A mixture of pleasure, relief, and anger moved through her.

"Don't cry out, please," he said from the floor. He lay on his back for a very long time before rolling onto his hands and knees, groaning.

"Are you injured?" She scrambled out of bed to his side in a thrice. The noise he created when he entered should have brought the servants straight to her room.

"You do care," he gasped with relief.

She'd never admit it to him. Catherine sat back, leaned away from him, then stood. "I am not a bit concerned. You may have broken a leg for all I care." She would have known that in an instant. He would have been howling in pain.

He pushed himself off the floor with both hands and crouched in a most unstealthly manner. "Truth be told . . ." He paused, looking up at her. She held her breath. "I am half mad since you've gone. Nothing has been the same without you."

Catherine couldn't believe what she heard. Nothing he said could have pleased her more but she couldn't let on that she felt the same. Retaining her composure, she studied what she could see of his expression. The pained look on his face and the longing in his eyes, together with the uncertainty in his voice, were very convincing.

"You should not be here, my lord." It struck her how improper entertaining him in her nightrail was. She stood between her bed, where she'd find a modest wrap, and the door, to exit, wondering which direction was best.

"Haverton—please." He moved to her side and covered her hands with his. "You must call me Haverton. No, call me Robert—Catherine."

"I will call your mother," she warned, moving away toward the door.

"No, don't leave," he pleaded, stepping toward the door, toward her. He reached out to block her departure.

She moved past him, back toward her bed and his hand brushed the arm of her nightrail. Catherine snatched up a blanket and held it in front of her.

"Please. I don't want you to send me away." His expression was one of anguish and the sadness in his voice brought her near tears.

Having him near was torture. She didn't want him to leave either. She moved away from the bed, a little closer to the door. The blanket she'd used to conceal her modesty trailed behind. "What do you think you are doing by coming here?"

"I had to see you."

Was it her imagination or did Haverton's—Robert's— voice hold a quaver of desperation. "It is customary to use the front door, and usually during daylight hours."

"I–I–"

"You don't want anyone to know you're here, do you?" By his look of astonishment, she knew she had either stumbled onto his thinly veiled scheme or had been completely wrong about his intentions. The very next moment, she decided the latter not to be true.

"You've already refused me an audience this night. I doubt you would have agreed to any time I cared to call." He smiled, it was a tentative one. "Please, I wanted—needed to see you." He held out his hand to her. His presence frightened her a little but she couldn't deny that she had missed him.

His second step brought him closer and a freshly brewed bout of apprehension rose within her. She tried to pull away but he stood on the corner of the blanket. Catherine slipped, losing her balance. He wrapped his arms around her, trying to steady her but it came too late. In a matter of moments she headed to the floor, bringing the Marquess tumbling along.

Haverton wrapped his arms around her, holding her close, protecting her, absorbing the impact of their landing. Catherine gave a small cry when the wind was knocked out of her.

"Are you hurt? Catherine—are you all right?"

She nodded. Partly from the lack of air, and partly from having his face an inch away from hers. He was too close. Not too close, she hoped, to resist. He lay next to, and against her, on the Persian carpet.

"I'm dreadfully sorry." But there was some amuse-ment in his voice, as if he knew that since no harm had come to either one of them, he could enjoy their misfortune.

"It was an accident," she replied, remaining still. Catherine had no wish to move because that would cause him to move, which is exactly what she wished to avoid—movement of any sort, toward or away from her.

"No. Not about this," he said. She could hear the faint smile in his voice. He tightened his arms about her. "I must apologize to you about the other—the other night. I should not have kissed you."

"You are not only to blame. I was foolish, I allowed it to happen. I was a willing participant . . . but I was wrong." She began to struggle free, pushing against him to escape.

He held her tight but did not hurt or frighten her. "No, you weren't wrong," he persuaded her in a kind and gentle manner. "I should have known better. I would never wish to harm you, you must know that."

She had thought that . . . once.

"Catherine, I am lost without you." The ache in his words moved through her, making her soften toward him. She relaxed, enjoying his nearness as much as he relished hers.

"Don't you dare make me feel sorry for you, because I don't." Anger tainted Catherine's words and the darkness did not disguise the tremor in her voice. "You could have your choice of any lady of the *ton* with a crook of your finger—why do you return to me?"

Haverton didn't answer. Instead he laid his hand on her head lightly, smoothing her hair. He drew a strand of hair through his fingers and pressed the end to his lips. The gesture touched her and sent a tingle straight down to her toes. She closed her eyes and, as much as it pained her, told herself it didn't matter. No matter what he did, he couldn't have her.

After turning the corner on the second-story landing, the Duchess of Waverly, with Simon not two steps behind, stopped in front of the third room on the right, turned the knob, and pushed the door open.

"Mother!" Robert cried, pushing himself upright as she stepped through the bedchamber door. "This isn't what it looks like," he went on to explain, rather ineffectively, the Duchess thought, and finally proclaimed, "I'm afraid this is exactly what it looks like."

"Haverton—I mean . . . his lordship slipped on the blanket, Your Grace, and we both fell." Catherine made her attempt to justify their awkward circumstances.

After standing solidly on his own two feet, Robert helped Catherine to hers. It was nice to see that even after being caught in an uncomfortable situation, he was still a gentleman.

"You cannot sneak into my house, rendezvous with my lady's companion and simply walk away." She glared at her elder son.

"We were merely—"

"I saw what I saw. I will not have any 'merely' going

on in my house." A stern performance would serve the Duchess well and she kept her excitement contained. "What you do in your household is one thing, what you do in mine is quite another. This time there are consequences."

"What consequences?" Catherine asked Robert.

It was nice to see Catherine look to Robert for guidance.

"You must marry—at once! You have been hopelessly compromised."

"I say, Robert. I think she means it," Simon chimed in during the Duchess' pause.

"Marriage?" Catherine gasped.

"You cannot expect me to simply ignore that I found you and my son cavorting on the floor of your bedchamber," the Duchess directed at Catherine.

"We fell, Your Grace, it was an accident."

"There are no *accidents* in my house." That may have been true but Catherine and Robert acted and looked quite guilty.

"I am more than happy to do what is required." Haverton's expression told a different story. He did not look displeased at all. "I think we should remove to more . . . accommodating surroundings. Shall we say the parlor in twenty minutes?"

"You need time to dress, my dear," the Duchess said to Catherine and then glanced at Robert who gazed lovingly at Catherine. "Make that ten and I expect to see you in less than five, Robert."

The Duchess pushed Simon into the hallway and closed the door.

"You knew exactly what was going on, didn't you, Mother?" Simon was pale.

"I would think arriving any later might have proved embarrassing and any earlier would have not given your brother enough time to have made his intent clear."

"He's in love with her, you know."

"And that"—the Duchess glanced at her youngest son over her shoulder—"is all the more reason why they should wed."

Chapter Eleven

Five minutes later, Catherine and Haverton entered the drawing room where Simon and the Duchess of Waverly waited. She sat to one side of the sofa and Haverton sat next to her. The Duchess, sitting across from them, appeared quite serious and glanced from Catherine to Haverton.

"Let's not waste time, shall we? We've important arrangements to make. Come closer, children." The Duchess beckoned the three near. "This is what we shall do . . . Robert. After your public introduction to Catherine, it will be your task to convince the mothers of every single young woman of our fair city that you are about to be taken off the marriage mart by courting her openly."

"I shall be more than willingly do my part." Haverton

smiled, wide-eyed, and it seemed to Catherine he was honestly pleased to do as his mother suggested.

"I cannot tell you how glad I am to hear that." She produced a soft smile of her own. "And you, Catherine, must be accepted as an eligible bride for Robert."

"I don't think anyone will accept me." Catherine could not exactly see how this would all work out. "What will happen when they discover he is to marry his chaperone?"

"You must understand, my dear, servants blend into the background. Trust me, no one really took notice of you as Robert's chaperone. We shall style your hair, alter your gowns so you can take your rightful place as a lady of quality."

However did the Duchess know?

"It is the least I can do for my namesake," the Duchess confessed.

"Are you Kate . . . Kate Marlowe?" Catherine could not believe that this was possible. "My mother's childhood friend?"

"Yes, I am." The Duchess' smile broadened. "Your mother Emily and I lived on neighboring estates."

That explained why she had always been so kind to Catherine and her family.

"Robert is not to wed his chaperone. He is to marry my goddaughter, the late Earl Thornton's granddaughter."

"An earl's granddaughter?" Simon brightened. "She's a lady? I never doubted it for a moment."

Haverton looked from his mother to Catherine. "Is this true? Your grandfather, an earl?"

"Yes, he passed away seven years ago. Then we were turned out by the countess. Not my grandmother but his second wife. She'd have nothing to do with Mother and her four girls. We had difficulties at first. I don't know how we would have managed if Her Grace hadn't brought me here and found me a position as governess."

Catherine had never imagined the Duchess had been her mother's great friend. She'd seen her name on countless letters since she was a child.

"There was very little your mother would accept from me."

"You found me a job. I was able to send money to help my family but now . . . now . . . ." She was disgraced, Catherine could not help but look toward the Marquess. "I do not know how I am to—"

"That is all in the past now, my dear. We must move forward." There was an urgency to the Duchess' tone. "In a few days' time, I shall introduce Miss Catherine Hayward to the *ton* and after a whirlwind courtship, you and Robert shall marry."

"Why ever would I object?" Haverton responded some nights later at Almack's. "That's the third time you've asked that question in three days."

"This is the big night. You're to be introduced to her."

Simon did not need to remind him. "You still have a chance to back out."

"We've already been through this. I have no intention of backing out."

"Don't you feel as if you're being forced into this?" Simon no more understood the Marquess' feelings for Catherine than Haverton did.

All Haverton knew was he loved her.

"Mother is not forcing me, Simon. I choose to marry Catherine. She is the only woman I desire." With his mother's blessing for the marriage, the Marquess was guaranteed that Catherine couldn't back out either.

"Can you honestly tell me you don't care that Mother has plotted against you?"

"Simon." Haverton smiled and clapped his brother's shoulder. "Didn't you know, our mother is always plotting against us."

"Not me, she isn't."

"You're heir presumptive," Haverton reminded him. "Unless I marry and start filling the nursery soon, I suspect in two years' time she would have turned all of her efforts on you."

An expression of surprise then relief swept over Simon's face. He must have just realized with his brother's upcoming nuptials that he'd dodged that bullet. "I had no idea."

"I have nothing to fear from Mother. I've always been able to spot a trap at fifty paces." Haverton didn't care in the least if his mother had manipulated him, Catherine, or their present situation. All Haverton cared about was that he would be with Catherine.

No one seemed to recognize her when she entered Almack's. Catherine wasn't surprised. Even she hadn't recognized herself the first time she stepped in front of the glass after the hairdresser and seamstress had worked their magic.

Her shoulder-length, light-brown hair now shimmered with golden streaks. A fringe of hair wisped over her forehead and soft ringlets nearly covered her head.

Even the yards of ribbon around her shoulders did not replace the missing three inches of neckline. However, Her Grace was right, if Catherine wished to blend in she had to wear what was in fashion.

As she entered the hallowed halls that evening, Catherine caught whispers of, "She's the Duchess of Waverly's goddaughter" and "the granddaughter of the late Earl Thornton." Their unexpected ten-minute appearance at Madame Suchet's had done exactly what the Duchess had expected. Tonight everyone knew exactly who Catherine was and what she was doing here . . . or *thought* they knew.

By the time Catherine had reached the ballroom, her dance card was filled and she was turning down partners. The women squinted at her, looking green with envy. The gentlemen were ever so gracious and bowed lower than she had seen before.

"There he is," the Duchess whispered to her from

behind a fan. "No, don't look, my dear." Her Grace laid her hand upon Catherine's arm, staying any motion. "You mustn't appear anxious. Let Robert come to you."

Haverton saw them entering, and for a moment was speechless. Dressed in a white silk gown with a flowing overskirt that billowed around her, she looked as if she floated on a cloud.

"Didn't tell me, old man, that your mother was coming with an angel," Sir Giles said to Haverton before addressing Fitzgerald. "What do you think?"

Although out of breath, the Marquess finally managed to whisper, "Gentlemen, Cupid's arrow has found its mark. I am in love." How Catherine had managed to look lovelier was beyond him.

She'd been beautiful in her modest gowns. The way she wore her hair in a tight bun showed the whole perfection of her face. Dressed in modern day finery as she was tonight, Catherine was simply breathtaking.

A halo of golden hair framed her face with soft curls and ringlets dancing about her neck. Soft, feathering curls teased her cheeks and jaw, masking the perfection that lay beneath, adding a sense of mystery.

"Love?" Sir Giles gasped in disbelief. "The deuce, man—have you lost your senses?"

"There go our chances," Fitzgerald quipped.

"My heart is completely and utterly lost." Placing his hand on his chest, the Marquess struck what he hoped was a memorable pose.

Sir Giles nudged Fitzgerald in the ribs. "Best have an

introduction before Haverton steps in—we'll have a dance with her at least."

"Right," Fitzgerald agreed. The two hurried to join the admirers gathering around the Duchess and her ward.

Haverton had always thought Catherine beautiful but now the crowd around her told him he was not the only man who thought so. Her admirers parted as he neared. He was quite aware that everyone watched him, them, in their first public exchange.

"There isn't any chance you've a dance left on your card for me, is there?"

"I'm sorry." Catherine flashed him a small, shy, self-conscious smile. "No."

"I thought not." Haverton glanced down, feeling a bit self-conscious himself. "Then I will have to be satisfied with seeing you tomorrow morning."

"Tomorrow morning? Shouldn't you call in the afternoon?"

"Perhaps so but there must be some benefit to being the son of your godmother." He leaned closer to whisper, "I'd like to have you all to myself before your admirers arrive and trip all over themselves."

The smile she bestowed upon him was luminous. "Then I shall look forward to your visit." Catherine glanced over Haverton's shoulder and he knew behind him waited a gentleman to take his place. The Marquess bowed over her hand and stepped back, allowing Lord Dobson to claim his dance.

Haverton watched Lord Dobson lead Catherine to the dance floor. Tonight, he realized, she was not his alone. For the first time in his life, Haverton had to share—and he did not like the notion in the least.

"She is quite lovely, don't you think?" Celeste brushed against Haverton's sleeve and wound her arm through his. "But your taste never ran toward school-room misses, did they?"

He was quite sure she wanted to make sure his attention was obligatory, not genuine. "I must do my part to guarantee she's a success. After all, she is my mother's goddaughter."

"And with approval from you, she will be accepted throughout the *ton*, no doubt."

"No doubt." His feigned lack of interest in Catherine might fool the other guests but he felt certain it would not convince Celeste. She knew that look of interest in his eyes all too well. There would be no hiding his true feelings from her.

"Shall I partner you on the dance floor and repair your reputation, madam?"

Celeste slapped him on his sleeve with her closed fan for teasing her and smiled. "As if my reputation needed repair."

He returned her smile and offered, "Perhaps a dance for old time's sake?"

"Yes, for old time's sake." Haverton escorted Celeste to the dance floor.

* * *

After the party, Haverton returned to Moreland Manor and stepped into his library, ending the most perfect evening. "I don't believe I have ever seen anyone more beautiful." He couldn't get the image of Catherine out of his mind.

Simon pulled off his jacket, loosened his cravat, and flopped into a winged-back chair, looking completely wretched. "There wasn't a chance to have a single word with her all night."

"Don't take it personally. There were many who never had a chance. Dance card was full, don't you know." Haverton sat in the chair next to his brother. "What a crush! Even if I wanted a *tete-a-tete* it would never have happened. Did you see that line?"

He had danced several sets with other eligible ladies to give the illusion he was taking the notion of seriously searching for a wife.

Simon stabbed an accusing finger at him. "You want her for yourself, don't you?"

Haverton straightened, a bit taken aback by his brother's hostile tone. "I thought that was the whole idea." Simon was present when their mother had brought up the plan to present Catherine at Almack's.

"You needn't bring up the fact that no one but you is good enough for her. It's not true, you know."

"What the devil is wrong with you?" Haverton sat forward, thinking perhaps his brother had gone mad.

"Nothing's wrong with me." Simon turned away, his voice choked with emotion. "Just because you have a dance with her, you think the two of you are betrothed or something equally as ridiculous."

Haverton took exception to this accusation. "I beg your pardon. Haven't I just told you that I did not dance with Catherine, her dance card was full."

"Catherine? Why are you bringing her up?" If it was possible, Simon grew angrier.

"That is the lady to which I am referring. Who are you talking about?"

Simon sat quietly before his answer came forth. "Lady Honoria."

"Honoria Darlington?" It was fortunate Haverton was already seated, he might have fallen over at the news.

A curt nod was Simon's answer.

"I don't believe it, you're in love with her." By God, he was, Haverton realized. And he knew the signs of a man in love well. The thought of Honoria Darlington— no, he didn't want to think about her. "She's been after me, you know."

Simon stared at his elder brother in amazement. "It's not her, it's her mother. She only has eyes for you—her mother that is, not Honoria. Lady Darlington won't hear of anyone under the rank of an earl paying court to her daughter. That leaves me out in the cold."

"Of course. Why should she not?" Haverton offered in his usual cool tone. "Is she not sweet, beautiful, and charming? And her kisses, that of an angel's." That's how he had described Catherine. Would Simon believe his beloved had any fewer qualities?

Simon straightened in alarm. "You do want her for yourself!"

"Lady Honoria?" Haverton stood, stepping away from Simon and heading for his desk. "Heavens, no."

"What's all this talk of her being a sweet, charming girl about then?"

Simon's infatuation with her was worse than the Marquess had thought. Haverton couldn't even make a joke about it. This younger brother was serious about his feelings for Honoria, and he was clearly jealous.

"I am sympathizing with you." Haverton sat on the edge of his desk. "I know exactly what you're going through. I thought life had come to an end when Mother took Catherine away. Don't you remember? I was miserable."

The despondent look in Simon's eyes told Haverton that he remembered and that he, too, had experienced the same.

"I wouldn't wish the same for you. If only . . . if only . . ." An idea began to grow. "Perhaps there is something I can do to help the two of you."

"Help us?" Interested, Simon abandoned his chair and approached his brother. "What do you have in mind?"

Haverton thrummed his fingers on the surface of the desk, wondering if deviousness ran in the family—if it did, he was certain it was from the maternal side.

"I will pretend to court Honoria," Haverton proposed.

"Exactly how will your pretending to court Honoria help me?"

Did Haverton imagine that look in Simon's eyes? Or did he still believe the Marquess wanted her all to himself? "Her mother will see me, not you, call for Honoria. What she won't see is the Moreland brothers changing places in a location of our choosing."

"Yes, I see." A conspiratorial spark glinted in Simon's eye.

Sitting at his desk, Haverton pulled a sheet of paper from his drawer and penned a note. "How's a drive this afternoon sound?"

"Today?" Clearly Simon was not prepared for this immediate action.

"I'd wager that if I made you wait to see her a single hour more than necessary it would drive you straight to Bedlam."

"You *do* understand."

"I'd best be off to bed if I were you. I imagine you'd wish to look your best for Honoria." Haverton smiled. "Not that she would ever think less of you with dark circles rimming your eyes."

"To bed, yes, that sounds excellent." Simon ran around the desk to shake his brother's hand. "This is wonderful. You can't imagine what this means to me, Robert."

"I think I do." If only courting Catherine had been this easy. The way things were going, he'd never had a chance to court her at all. "I'll have this delivered in the morning," indicating the note. "I'll meet you at the corner of Park and Green Streets at half past three. And there, my dear brother, you shall see your beloved Honoria." Haverton nudged Simon away. "Now off with you."

"I shan't sleep a wink, I tell you." Simon pulled open the door to leave. "Not one wink."

Simon wouldn't be the only one, Haverton mused. He was to see Catherine soon. Alone. He, too, was far from sleep. What was he ever going to do to pass the time until then?

What an exquisite display of flora. The Duchess of Waverly had never seen so many flowers in her house. Roses in various colors of red, pink, and white, pure white hothouse gardenias by the dozen, and camellias of various hues were some of the few she could readily recognize. Which of these tributes to Catherine was from Robert, the Duchess wondered. What would this *Rogue of the Realm*, as she had heard him frequently referred to, send the woman he was to marry?

"Oh, my!" Catherine stood at the foot of the stairs and held onto the post to steady her from the amazing sight below. "Where did all these flowers come from?"

"Your many admirers, my dear." The Duchess understood that Catherine had no notion of the social rituals.

"Admirers? But there are so many." Nor did Catherine recognize how much of a success she was.

"If Robert's not careful, you may change your mind about marrying him and decide on someone else."

Catherine blushed. "I hardly think that is possible."

The Duchess smiled, her comment was all in fun. "Of course not. We both know how you feel, am I correct?"

Catherine's shy smile told the Duchess everything she needed to know. This young woman was, indeed, in love with her son. She motioned to Catherine to come near.

"Shall we take a closer look?"

Catherine pulled the card from a bunch of violets sitting low on the table, almost hidden by the thick, leafy green neighbors. "This is from Lord Peter Drysdale."

"Drysdale, you say?" The Duchess was neither impressed by Lord Peter nor his offering of violets. She extracted a card from a tall arrangement of red roses. The card was from Sir Samuel Allensby. She didn't think much of Allensby but his offering was more of what the Duchess had in mind. Nothing was too good for her goddaughter.

"These orchids are from William, Lord Tetridge," Catherine read another.

Orchids from Lord Tetridge? That was very well done of him. Very well done. The Duchess had never seen such a collection of exquisite, exotic blooms in her life.

Catherine opened a small box and tears welled in her eyes.

"What is that?" the Duchess asked, most anxious to know who had had the audacity to send a gift.

"Honeysuckle," Catherine whispered, holding the lavender-colored, ribbon-bound sprigs to her nose. "It's from Haverton."

"Honeysuckle? Why on earth would he . . ." the Duchess groaned. "I would have thought Robert would have more sense in that pretty head of his than to send a common—" She was halted by the tears trickling down Catherine's cheeks.

The image of Catherine inhaling the pink and yellow flowers with her eyes closed and a smile of contentment made the Duchess take back every word.

Judging from Catherine's reaction to his offering, Robert knew exactly what he was doing.

Catherine couldn't believe Haverton had remembered her fondness for honeysuckle over roses. Its presence certainly had caught her off guard. It seemed as if ages had passed since they'd walked in his garden and she had confessed a preference for them.

Male voices in the foyer caught her attention.

"Compose yourself. Robert's here."

Catherine sniffed and wiped her eyes only moments before Haverton stepped into the room. His eyes brightened when he spotted her.

Haverton greeted his mother first and kissed her hand. Continuing past her, he reached out to Catherine. "My dear," he murmured no louder than a whisper. The smile on his face reflected genuine pleasure. "Your touch makes my hollow existence whole again." He refused to release her hand and drew her near. She willingly went.

"Your mother is present," Catherine cautioned him.

"She knows what I've had to withstand and I'm sure

she'll allow us a bit of privacy." He glanced at her from under an arched brow.

"Of course, dear," Her Grace replied. "But remember, you are not as yet wed. So do take care."

"I promise to behave myself." He smiled and laid Catherine's hand through his arm, escorting her from the room to the adjoining terrace where he merely gazed at her.

"What is it? Why are you staring at me?"

"I apologize. It's just that I am simply amazed at your transformation."

Had it not pleased him? Had he preferred the drab long brown hair and serge she wore to the new golden locks, lace, and silk?

"I'm not complaining in the least, but when I look at you I no longer see *Mrs. Hayes.*"

"No? Who do you see?" She hoped he wasn't disappointed. Catherine had tried her best to represent the socially acceptable woman he would be expected to marry.

He took a moment longer to regard her. "There is a remarkable air of confidence about you. You have the bearing and poise of a different woman. Wherever did she come from?"

"I'm sure I don't know. Do you disapprove?"

"I think she might have been hiding under a pair of spectacles and a tight bun." Haverton leaned closer and whispered. "I must admit I am glad she's decided to come out and make herself known."

Had she changed that much? Catherine wouldn't have believed there would be such a marked difference by altering only her hair and wardrobe.

"I could hardly wait for the hours to pass until I saw you again. I had hoped to fall asleep last night, at least for a few hours, but I couldn't. I stepped outside and strolled the path by the rose garden. Do you remember? You had the misfortune of getting your skirts tangled, and I had the good fortune to help you free yourself, and in turn, help myself to a glimpse of your shapely ankle."

Catherine gasped. "You did not peek!"

"I'm afraid I did." His self-conscious smile betrayed the embarrassment of his confession.

"And I thought you were a gentleman."

"Don't ask me why but I feel closer to you when I'm in the garden. This morning the breeze carried the scent of honeysuckle and I remembered you saying how much you loved its sweet fragrance."

He truly had remembered.

"I procured a few sprigs, found a bit of your ribbon to bind the stems and sent them with my warmest regards."

My ribbon? Catherine thought she'd recognized it. It had been hers. One that, no doubt, had been inadvertently left behind.

"I can hardly wait for the day we are married and settled comfortably into Moreland Manor. Your absence is most greatly felt. How I long to gaze at you across the breakfast table and sketch your likeness in the evenings while you sew. I've missed our afternoon strolls in the garden," he announced, as if the time since their last walk had been an eternity.

"We only had but one," she reminded him, trying not laugh.

"Nevertheless I look forward to making a turn about the garden our daily routine. And how I've missed hearing you play."

"Play?" Catherine had to think a bit. "Oh, practicing on the pianoforte."

"I miss hearing your music more than I ever thought was possible."

"If you could call that music. I play horribly." Catherine had nearly forgotten she'd spent time at the keyboard. Only a few hours, in fact, practicing the piece Simon had given her.

"Nonsense, I thought you were progressing quite splendidly."

"You are too kind," she replied before realizing that the Marquess of Haverton was never overly kind to anyone. For him to make such an exception for her would mean that she, Catherine, was not just anyone to him.

Chapter Twelve

Lady Darlington observed the Marquess of Haverton's seal upon the proffered note and could barely maintain her usual composure but did so until the footman left the breakfast room. Breaking the missive open, she scanned the contents and screeched with joy, blubbering excitedly, unable to utter a single word.

"Mama, Mama, what is it?" Honoria's cup of hot chocolate slipped from her fingers and dropped onto its saucer.

Lady Darlington snatched her linen napkin off her lap and dropped it on the table next to her empty plate. "Oh, my dear! Oh, my dear! This is the best possible news."

"Mama?"

"Quickly—we must make haste—you must be ready!" Lady Darlington pushed away from the table and rushed to Honoria, prying her away from her seat. "Come now, we must see to your toilette."

"But Mama, I have just finished my morning toilette," Honoria answered as her mother ushered her out of the breakfast room into the hallway.

"There is no time to waste, he will be here soon."

"Who? Who is coming?"

"Don't dawdle, girl. We must make haste. Your hair must shine—it must have at least a thousand strokes of the brush."

Honoria stood at the bottom of the stairs. "I shall not move another inch until you tell me what is happening."

Lady Darlington threw her hands up. "It is the Marquess of Haverton—he will arrive at three to take you driving."

Honoria blanched.

"I can hardly believe it. My little Honoria and Lord Haverton at Hyde Park for all to see." She pulled a concealed handkerchief from her sleeve and dabbed at her eyes. "I am so very happy."

"Lord Haverton is calling? Here? For me?"

"His note says he will arrive at three in the afternoon to take you driving. How this happened, I do not know, but I will not question my good fortune."

"Yes, I must go to my room." She raced up the stairs, outrunning her mother.

Finally the girl was seeing the right of the matter. Was it possible she had changed her mind about the Marquess? She seemed to be quite anxious about his call.

"Wear your new chip bonnet, the one with the pale blue ribbons. It will show off your eyes to perfection."

After reaching her room, Honoria faced her mother. "I will not step foot out of this room."

"What did you say?" Lady Darlington had worked very hard to this end. She was not about to let her bird-witted, upstart of a daughter stand in her way of claiming the Marquess.

"I said, I refuse." Honoria planted herself on the bed and crossed her arms. "I will not see him."

Lady Darlington stepped toward her daughter and threatened, "You will do as you are told."

"I am so very pleased that you accepted my invitation on such short notice, Lady Honoria." Haverton bowed over her hand, doing his utmost to portray the ideal suitor, and kept in mind that his brother would probably thrash him if he did not behave as a gentleman should.

"She is quite honored that you should ask, my lord," Lady Darlington answered for her daughter. "I had no idea you had the least bit of interest in my little Honoria."

It was quite clear to Haverton that Lady Darlington was trying her utmost not to appear overly pleased. If the Countess had the slightest notion of the real reason he was here, she'd have thrown him out and slammed the door in his face. The only person Haverton intended to please was Simon.

Within ten minutes, Honoria sat next to the Marquess and they were on their way to the intersection of Park and Green Streets. Where, unbeknownst to Honoria, her afternoon drive in the park would take a dramatic turn for the better. Or so Haverton hoped.

The chit was sulking. What did Simon see in this girl? How he could have fallen for this timid mouse, Haverton would never understand. She hadn't made so much as a sound or acknowledged his presence since they had started. How inexplicably rude.

"Ah, here we are now, my pet." Haverton brought the curricle to a halt and Simon ran out to greet them.

"Simon!" Honoria cried in complete shock. "Whatever are you doing here?"

Haverton climbed out, leaving the ribbons and forthcoming explanation to his brother.

Simon greeted Honoria with a kiss to her hand and settled into the driver's seat next to her. "I'm sorry there wasn't time to explain but this is all Haverton's idea. He knew your mother wouldn't allow me to call on you so he thought he might call on you himself and after your mother watched you leave in his care, I would take his place."

"That is absolutely brilliant!" Honoria pronounced.

"I wish you to remember, Simon. She is in my care," Haverton cautioned.

"Do not worry, I would never let anything harm Honoria." Simon gazed into her wide, blue eyes.

Haverton cleared his throat, interrupting the couple's

mooning. "Shall I meet you back here in, let's say, an hour?"

"An hour it is, and thank you again, Robert." Simon picked up the ribbons and signaled the horses forward.

"Thank you so much, Lord Haverton." Honoria waved good-bye.

Haverton watched them leave. Was there nothing more delightful than seeing two people in love?

The Duchess was elated, although it was not completely unexpected, that Catherine was so popular in society. Tonight at the Stoddard's ball, she held court with no fewer than five young men, all vying for her attention. What Her Grace wanted to know was why Robert was not one of them. His presence would chase the young bucks off in an instant.

"I trust you have saved a dance for Robert as I've instructed?" the Duchess inquired.

"Yes, Your Grace."

"It's about time he made his intentions known." Spotting her younger son among the guests in the crowd, the Duchess of Waverly set out in his direction while continuing to scan the room for her eldest.

With a rap of her closed fan upon his shoulder, she caught Simon's attention. "Where has that brother of yours gotten himself off to?"

"At the moment, he's dancing with Lady Honoria," Simon said with absolute calm and with more than a passing interest in the couple.

"Dancing with Honoria Darlington?" the Duchess gasped outraged. She spotted them on the dance floor and muttered, "That simpering, empty-headed—"

"Mother, Lady Honoria is a most agreeable young lady."

The Duchess swung her gaze from Robert and turned a skeptical eye onto Simon. Did he think so, indeed? She detected something more going on here but she did not have time to concern herself with his apparent interest at present.

What did Robert think he was doing? By ignoring Catherine and dancing with the Darlington girl he would give everyone the wrong impression. She would box his ears for this. She might ring a peal over his head for this behavior but she doubted he would pay any notice to that, either.

The Duchess glanced over her shoulder. Catherine stood nearby and, by the expression she wore, had heard everything. Robert was not the only one to be scolded for errors. The Duchess realized she had made a mistake by allowing Catherine to see.

"I find it very hard to believe that even Robert would be heartless enough to treat you in such a manner," Her Grace remarked.

Catherine said nothing.

"You cannot allow him to continue on this way."

"I have no hold over him, Your Grace. He is free to do as he wishes."

The Duchess caught Catherine's cool expression.

"You are mistaken, my dear. To the *ton*, Robert may appear to be unattached but we know better, do we not?"

Again Catherine said nothing.

"If he insists on straying, I can only suggest that you are free to do the same. As we have discussed this afternoon, you have plenty of suitors. May I suggest you pay particular attention to Lord Tetridge or Sir Alex Pemberton. Robert should do well to have a taste of his own medicine."

The Duchess could tell that her tactics did not please Catherine. She wasn't even sure if the girl would entertain the notion of stringing the suitors along to capture Robert's attention.

"I want you to tell your elder brother that his mother, the Duchess, would like a word with him," she informed Simon after Catherine had stepped away.

Lady Darlington stood to one side of the dance floor, smiling as she watched Haverton dance with her daughter. Counting her chickens before they hatched was a dangerous thing to do—and the Duchess of Waverly would bet Lady Darlington was doing exactly that.

She'd heard gossip about Haverton and Lady Honoria—but it wasn't true. He had promised to marry Catherine—he said himself he was in love with her.

So what did Robert think he was doing?

"How is the courtship progressing?" Haverton asked while on the dance floor with Honoria.

"Mother still has the notion you are courting me," she admitted, less shyly.

"It would serve us best if you allowed her to go on believing just that."

Honoria nodded. The shine of love sparkled in her eyes. Love for Simon. Haverton knew it was love, he had seen the same shimmer in Catherine's eyes when she looked at him.

"Now that we have shared a dance, I imagine you can expect me to call on you tomorrow afternoon. Shall we say the same time?"

Honoria blushed and smiled, gazing demurely up at him. "Yes, nothing would please me more. I cannot wait until I see Simon again. Until tomorrow."

Simon stood to one side for Haverton, acknowledging Honoria with a smile and a nod of his head. "I am here to deliver a message from Mother."

"Uh, oh."

"Your mother, the Duchess, wishes a word. I believe she means to put the fear of God into you. You've done something to displease her, all right."

"Too late to put things to right, I'll wager. Well there's nothing to be done about it now. I might as well see what she wants."

Simon caught Haverton by the arm. "Have you made the arrangements with Honoria?"

"Do not fret. The arrangements for tomorrow"—he smiled—"have been taken care of."

* * *

Catherine strolled by the chaperones' corner, the place she usually spent her time while at these functions, and slowed to hear what they were saying.

"My dear Miss Trueblood, have you heard about Lady Henrietta?" said the one Catherine recognized as Miss Price.

"What is it?" Miss Trueblood inquired. "What have you heard?"

"I have heard that Miss Henrietta Lonsdale has set her cap for the Marquess of Haverton."

Miss Price and Miss Trueblood shared an enjoyable laugh. Mrs. Baldwin did not look pleased.

"Any one of these lovely young ladies could make do as his marchioness—but who could keep hold on him as husband?" Miss Trueblood continued.

"As if he could be truly the least bit interested in her." The knowing looks and understanding nods of their heads replaced the matrons' girlish giggles of only moments ago.

"True—very true, Miss Trueblood."

"Lady Darlington and I believe that our Honoria would make a splendid marchioness," said Mrs. Baldwin.

"There is nothing wrong with your charge, mind you." Miss Trueblood placed a comforting hand upon Mrs. Baldwin. "If one wishes to become Lady Haverton, one must become accustomed to Haverton's nature."

"And his nature being?" Miss Price inquired.

"He is a man who cannot remain faithful to one woman. It would be impossible for him, I fear."

"Outrageous!" Mrs. Baldwin exclaimed. Her face became as red as her hair. "What if he were to fall in love?"

"Gracious, Lord Haverton fall in love?" Miss Price did not sound hopeful at the prospect. "He is a man! Do you think men believe in such things?"

"I cannot imagine," Miss Trueblood remarked. "I am not sure if I believe in such a thing."

Miss Price continued. "Yes, I'm afraid the young lady who manages to get Lord Haverton to the sticking point may have his name, his title, and his children but still may yet to have his heart. It is a sad thing."

"Sad for his wife, perhaps," said Miss Trueblood. "But not sad for the remaining female population of London."

Catherine gasped, her heart ached, thinking herself a fool again to believe that he loved her. She wished she had never overheard the trio. Was it truly impossible for Haverton to remain true to one woman?

"What do you think you are doing with that milk and water miss?" The Duchess did not allow Haverton a chance to answer and continued, "What of Catherine?"

At the mention of Catherine's name, Haverton smiled. Where was she? Ah, yes, there she stood, across the room holding court with a half dozen men. Knowing that not one of them, he mused, had the slightest chance with her. The lovely creature was his, all his.

"You are to be wooing her! How do you suppose it looks to have you off dancing with some insignificant chit? Are you not going to propose before the Season's end? Which, I might remind you, comes in a fortnight."

"Yes, Mother. I am very well aware of that."

"You don't seem to be . . . and you certainly don't act as if you *are* aware. I think it's high time you do something about your upcoming betrothal or else you won't have a betrothal to bother with. In the event that you might have changed your mind about her, do not worry, Catherine has her choice of several eligibles."

"Don't be silly, Mother, I am as devoted to her as I ever was. She is merely—" Haverton glanced back at Catherine and noted not a polite bearing, but her serious, interested expression in the men around her. It was one of . . . he looked closer and took note of her smile, of how her eyes sparkled as she conversed. Her fan dropped open and she swung away from the gentleman before her and peered over the top edge at him. Was she flirting?

By Gad, he would put a stop to this right now!

Haverton went to move past his mother, only to run into the barricade of her fan.

"Where do you think you are going?"

"I'm going to save Catherine from that swarm of preying men."

The Duchess looked over her shoulder. "I believe she is managing the situation quite well, considering."

"Considering what?"

"Considering she hasn't the experience of handling

men, other than yourself, that is. And I believe we can both agree that you are not like *most* men."

Haverton pushed the fan aside and growled through clenched teeth. "Do you expect me to stand here and watch her flirt with the Pinks of the *ton*? Make overtures to every eligible peer?"

"Well, I had not thought she would actually engage any of them . . ." The Duchess stared in Catherine's direction and feigned shock. "Oh dear, it appears that I am wrong. She is doing rather well, don't you think?"

"I do not want her doing *well* when it comes to engaging other men's attention." He leaned toward his mother and whispered, "Or had you forgotten she and I are to be married."

"Really?" Again his mother had the audacity to appear shocked. "One would not know it if they were to look at you. It appears that you have interests in a different quarter."

Is that how his behavior had looked to Catherine? Yes, he had danced, flirted, and pretended to court Honoria Darlington. That's what he wanted Honoria's mother to think. And that is no doubt what his own mother thought.

"I'd best clear up this mess." He must speak to Catherine at once. He needed to explain to her that it was for Simon's and Honoria's happiness. Haverton had to tell her immediately before the situation got out of hand.

"Good thinking—I knew you'd see the right of it."

The Duchess snapped her fan shut. "Swallow your anger and hurry along." She gave him an encouraging push with the tip of her fan.

Taking his mother's advice, Haverton waded among the throng, approaching the woman he loved.

"Lord Haverton," Catherine called out graciously and smiled.

He could tell it wasn't a real smile but one applied for the benefit of the guests. Catherine might not have had the practice the other ladies had but she had his mother to coach her.

He'd been told that, in her time, the Duchess had been the year's Incomparable. She had had three proposals the first week of her Season and no less than twenty by the time the Season had ended. She knew exactly how to make a man come up to scratch.

His mother was an amazing woman. It was a good thing she was on his side. The Duchess was on his side, wasn't she?

"Miss Hayward," Haverton called out. The men around Catherine parted, creating a clear path directly to her. Several of the men left, no doubt intimidated by the Marquess as competition for her attention. "Our dance is next, is it not?"

"I'm sorry, I've changed my mind. I do not care to dance. I am so very fatigued."

"A stroll about the room, perhaps?"

"No, thank you," she returned quite kindly.

"A breath of fresh air in the gardens?" She was going to turn him down again. *A word alone with you*, he mouthed.

"Is your chaperone present?"

"As always. She is a necessary evil," he answered with practiced calm.

"Then I accept." Catherine nodded.

After offering her his arm, he led her out of the room, and Mrs. Goddard followed.

"She tends to her task, no doubt?" Catherine asked, glancing at the woman trailing them.

Haverton signaled Mrs. Goddard not to follow. "Isn't she a fright?"

Catherine took a second look. "I find her quite an acceptable replacement."

Haverton stilled and gazed into her eyes. "Catherine, there is no replacing you."

"From what I have seen you've been trying very hard to do exactly that," she replied unconcerned. "You seem to find Lady Honoria quite enchanting."

"As to that, it's not what you believe."

Catherine's voice rose and turned sharp. "And what is it, precisely, am I to believe?"

"My affection for you remains unchanged. I am completely and utterly devoted to you."

"I see." She sounded thoughtful.

Did she not feel the same? Would she not respond to him in kind?

"It may very well appear as if I am interested in Lady

Honoria but the truth of the matter is, I am not." It seemed all very complex at the moment but if she would only take the time to hear him out.

"That is very interesting." But she did not seem to care in the least.

"If you would allow me a few minutes of your time to explain."

"I'm afraid I do not have the time" She turned away from him and faced into the ballroom. "I'll be dancing the next set with Sir Giles."

"Sir Giles? I thought you did not care to dance."

"I beg your pardon, I should have made myself clearer. I do not care to dance with *you*. And tomorrow I'm planning a drive with Sir Alex Pemberton in Hyde Park."

"Sir Alex?" Haverton could not believe what he was hearing. Pemberton the Popinjay? She couldn't possibly mean it. "But what of our whirlwind romance where you and I make a public show of falling madly in love?"

"It seems you are too busy courting Lady Honoria for that type of display." Catherine gave a little sigh. "I believe it appears that we only have a passing acquaintance—allowing my godmother is your mother."

"But we are to wed!" Haverton was outraged.

"Are we? I do not recall an announcement or even a proposal for that matter." She blinked, looking up, trying to bring such a memory to mind. "I believe until the time of my betrothal, I am free to do as I wish, with whom I wish. My chaperone is quite liberal-minded and suggests I enjoy myself."

Haverton could hardly believe what he was hearing. "Your chaperone?"

"Did you not know? My chaperone is the Duchess of Waverly."

The following afternoon, Haverton thought he saw Catherine stepping into the yellow high-perched phaeton in the drive of his mother's house. He must have been mistaken and wished he was closer for a better look.

Who the devil was that?

The yellow monstrosity pulled away, moving down the drive. What a disgrace—the high-flying, meddlesome, Sir Alex. Why would he be hovering about here? He had no business with Catherine.

Haverton stepped out when his rig came to a stop and headed for the house. "Mother! Mother?" He strolled through the front door. "Was that Pemberton?"

"Why yes, dear, it was he."

The Marquess' frustration began to build. Haverton felt as if he was a stranger coming to call, instead of her son. "Why does Catherine keep company with Pemberton?"

"Well, you see, I'm afraid she's become a bit disillusioned with you." Mother's demeanor was odd. "I'm afraid it's very clear to all of us that you are about to offer for another young woman."

"I have no intention of the sort."

"That's the difficult part of it, I'm afraid. Men just don't understand."

"Understand what?"

"That's exactly what I mean." She motioned to him with her gardening clippers. "You have no idea what you've done to drive Catherine away."

"Drive Catherine away? I've done no such thing. I adore her . . . she is my heart!" What was Mother talking about? Nothing could have been further from his mind. He thought of nothing but Catherine except for his little diversion to help his brother—he tried to explain all that to her last evening. She should have no doubt he was completely devoted to her, he had reassured her of his affections—except she was a bit put off when he mentioned—

"Lady Honoria . . ." the Duchess uttered painfully. "Oh, yes. I have noticed. Indeed, we have both noticed, Catherine and I. I fear we are not the only ones. Do you not know how this appears to others? Do you ever consider the feelings of anyone before you act?"

"Honoria means nothing to me. Catherine knows." Haverton had no idea anyone had thought his attention to this chit could be serious. Well, Honoria's mother perhaps but not his own mother. Catherine must know how much he cared for her.

Haverton glanced out the window, down the road where he watched his beloved drive off with another man. She did know, didn't she?

* * *

An hour and thirty-seven minutes later, not that he had been keeping track of the time, Haverton, who had waited in his mother's sitting room, heard Catherine's and Pemberton's return.

Haverton leaped out of the chair and stepped carefully toward the door, listening to their exchange. He should be prepared, he told himself, to come to Catherine's aid if that cad Pemberton should force his attention on her.

"Thank you kindly for the drive, Sir Alex," Catherine spoke softly.

"I am your humble servant," said Pemberton.

Haverton crossed his arms, leaned against the frame of the door and glanced toward the heavens. His short prayer was for a measure of patience, composure, or deliverance . . . in that order.

"If you are in need, please do not hesitate to call. I am at your complete disposal."

That's all Pemberton was good for . . . disposal.

The sound of the door closing told the Marquess of the bounder's departure. Haverton left the sitting room and headed down the hall toward his mother's voice.

"Here he is now, you see?" she said to Catherine.

"Oh, Lord Haverton?" Catherine's cool tone made him feel like an outsider too.

He was her betrothed!

"How kind of you to pay a call but it is getting late, isn't it?"

"Late? It's not too late to go for a drive with Pemberton but it's too late to have a word with me?" Hostility and outrage coated his words.

"I'm sure you can make some time to speak to Robert," the Duchess intervened.

"I suppose I could." Catherine stepped into the parlor and sat, waiting for him to follow.

He could hardly believe what he was hearing. What were these two doing? Why were they treating him in this horrendous manner?

He felt irritable, angry, and impatient. He wanted, needed, to clarify his association with Lady Honoria to Catherine. To make it clear, absolutely clear, that his interest and heart were hers—Catherine's, not Honoria's.

She'll laugh, he told himself. She is going to think this entire episode very humorous when I tell her about this whimsical turn of events. How he pretended to court Honoria on Simon's behalf, and it *appeared* that he was sincere.

"I thought I had made my intentions to you perfectly clear the other night," he began, feeling better about the direction of their conversation already. This matter would be cleared up in a thrice. "I believe a further explanation is in order."

"An explanation? You certainly owe no explanation to me and I do not owe you an explanation of any kind."

"I think I do need to clarify my actions as of late. As I said last evening, there has been a misinterpretation of my arrangement with Lady Honoria Darlington."

"Arrangement? Is that what you call it? An *arrangement*?"

"It is not even that."

"Do you deny courting her?" Catherine's tone was no longer unemotional.

Haverton didn't want to blurt it all out. He wanted to phrase his words carefully. "It may appear as if I am courting her but I'm not actually courting her. You see, it is Simon who is courting her."

"Lord Simon, you say? How very strange. I do not recall ever seeing him keeping her company." Concern crept between Catherine's words. "You cannot deny she's kept you occupied as of late."

"Occupied." He smiled. Planning Honoria's and Simon's courtship had kept him occupied, he couldn't very well deny that. "If you are to imply that I have been paying you less attention than I would have liked, you are correct."

"I imagine you are a bit overwrought," Catherine began in a voice of ultimate calm.

"That is true. I can assure you that *you* have been utmost in my mind. Not a minute goes by when I do not think of you."

"How flattering of you to say." She gazed toward her clasped hands and cleared her throat. "I cannot tell you how many times I've heard that phrase, just since last night. You, I'm afraid, have been the least convincing yet."

"But we are to be married!" How could she think him insincere?

"That is what you say. However, I cannot see how I could possibly come to that conclusion since you spend most of your time with Lady Honoria and merely *think* of me." She glanced off to the side as if she had come upon an idea. "Perhaps I shall think of you while I am dancing tomorrow night. I wonder if you might feel my affection while I'm in the arms of Lord Tetridge?"

There the conversation ended. Catherine was not laughing and Haverton did not find anything about his situation the least bit funny.

Chapter Thirteen

Lord Simon escorted Catherine to the Markham's water party the following Saturday afternoon. This was her first floating party, and the enormous barge was no less decorated than the finest ballroom in London. She watched the shrubs and trees move slowly away as the vessel traveled down the river.

Once aboard, the guests had no choice but to remain on board. Never was that so apparent as when Catherine came face to face with Haverton and Lady Honoria. There was an awkward moment until Lord Simon finally said, "May I have a word with you, Robert?"

The men excused themselves, leaving Catherine standing with Lady Honoria, who promptly broke into tears.

"I do not know what I am to do." Honoria wept into her lace handkerchief.

Catherine was at a loss of words herself. Why did Lady Honoria feel she could confide in someone she shared only a passing acquaintance?

"I am sorry to trouble you, Miss Hayward, but Lord Haverton has been most kind, and he has always spoken so highly of you. I thought . . . I might seek your advice."

The Marquess had spoken of her to Honoria?

"His lordship told me you know of our 'arrangement' and . . . oh, Miss Hayward, the short time Simon and I have had together is absolute heaven. If only it could go on . . ."

Lady Honoria and Lord Simon? Honoria transformed before Catherine's eyes from a girl to that of a young lady. A very unhappy young lady who was very much in love.

"If I wish to go on seeing him, the pretense must be that I continue to court his elder brother." Honoria wiped her tears and tucked her handkerchief away. "Mama is determined that I set my cap for Haverton— but I do not wish to have anything to do with him." Her eyes filled with tears again. "He frightens me."

Then it was true. All of it. Haverton had not abandoned Catherine for Honoria, he was merely aiding a couple in love.

"But Simon . . . Lord Simon has told me of his

affection, and my feelings are equally engaged." She caught her lower lip between her teeth. "I'm afraid"—her voice began to crack—"that I do not know what we are going to do." A new bout of tears began. "You know what it is like to have a secret. After all, you and Lord Haverton are secretly engaged."

Catherine felt the wind knocked out of her. "Where did you hear that?"

"He told me the two of you were a love match and you are to be married." Catherine saw Honoria's honesty shine from her blue eyes. "And of course I would never ever tell another soul."

"To tell the truth, it remains to be seen whether Haverton and I will wed." Catherine seriously questioned it. The Marquess' explanation had sounded unbelievable and she all but called him a liar to his face. But he had been telling the truth.

"I was under the impression he loves you very much. Do you no longer love him?"

"Well, I—" Catherine's head swam, she wasn't sure what or whom to believe anymore.

"From what I understand, you are the reason Lord Haverton is helping us. Simon told me his brother knew exactly how it felt to be without one's true love and did not wish us to suffer the same as he had. Simon and I cannot keep seeing one another in secret. We are bound to be discovered sooner or later. Will you not, please, Miss Hayward, help us?"

Catherine understood everything Honoria said and

felt the greatest sympathy for her situation and wished only the best for her and Lord Simon. When it came to matters of the heart, Catherine doubted she could be of any help to anyone, even herself.

Nearly an hour ago Haverton had arrived at the Darlington residence without his chaperone. Lady Darlington had gladly handed over Honoria for him to escort her to the Markham's water party, also without Mrs. Baldwin, her chaperone.

Upon arrival at the private dock, the Marquess had planned to meet Simon. He had not expected to see his brother escorting Catherine but he should have known better. The encounter on the water vessel had been a strained one. If it had not been for Simon asking for a word alone with him, who knew how long they would have been standing there frozen in an awkward tableau, staring at one another.

Once alone, Simon voiced concerns that he and Honoria were progressing quite splendidly with their courtship. However, to move on to the next phase, marriage, would prove difficult. Neither he nor Simon could come up with a suitable plan but Simon was correct—they could not continue in this manner.

How could Haverton arrange for a marriage for Simon and Honoria when he and Catherine were to wed within a fortnight? Within the week, if Haverton had his say. At present, it appeared doubtful they would marry at all, Catherine would not tolerate him. That tangle needed to be worked out. What more could he tell her than the truth? What more could he—

Catherine approached and claimed Haverton's full attention. Simon and Honoria came together and faded to one side.

"Honoria and Simon," was all Catherine said.

Haverton could see the forgiveness in her eyes. She understood what he'd told her and she had learned the truth from Lady Honoria.

"I did try to tell you."

"How could you expect me to believe you?" Both anger and humiliation vied for first expression across her beautiful face.

"Ah, but you do now, don't you?" Haverton could never, ever be untrue to her.

"Yes, my lord, I do." She offered him a smile which he gladly accepted. "I—"

"You need not say another word." Haverton held her hand to his chest and smiled. "I find this quite refreshing."

"What?"

"Your honesty. Instead of playing games, as my mother suggested, you address me directly—thus the entire difficulty between us has been cleared."

"I haven't the kill of a London Miss to wind you around my little finger." Catherine could never treat him in a ruthless fashion but he knew she held some power over him.

"Do not ever deny that ability." He kissed her hand.

She gazed back at him in such a peculiar manner. He couldn't come near to describing it. "What you possess is far more potent."

"And what is that?"

"The ability to make me fall in love with you."

The smile that crossed her face, her eyes, gave him the most wonderful feeling. He wanted to pull her into his arms right here, right now, in front of everyone and kiss her. Instead he pressed a kiss onto her hand.

"Am I to understand that we are still to wed?" she asked, timid.

"Oh, yes." His arm stole around her waist to draw her near. "The sooner we do so, the better."

Hand in hand, Simon and Honoria approached.

"We're making a run to Gretna, Robert," Simon announced with Honoria by his side.

"What? You can't mean it." Haverton looked from one to the other with disbelief.

"If we wish to be together, we must. It's the only way." Honoria voiced her own opinion. "Mama will never allow us to marry."

"Simon, please. What will Mother say? She'll be furious."

"I'm not you. She doesn't care a fig for—"

"Mother's not going to approve of this dashing-off-to-Gretna business. She'll make your Honoria a young widow." Haverton turned to Honoria. "Think of your family. If you elope, there will be a scandal. Our family will survive but yours . . . think of your mother." He hardly felt sympathy for Lady Darlington but a mother's wrath was not to be taken lightly.

"She will not be happy that I'm not to marry you, my lord." Honoria spoke to him more forcefully than ever before.

"You must return to London some day." Haverton wanted the couple to be happy but did not wish them to rush willy-nilly into marriage. "Think about this very carefully."

Worry creased their love-struck faces. Honoria and Simon had taken Haverton's words seriously.

"But we wish to marry. How can we—" they started together.

"What if . . . there was an offer for you?" Catherine suggested.

"Lady Darlington would never consider me an appropriate—" Simon sounded discouraged regarding his prospects.

"Not you." Catherine swatted at Simon's shoulder in playfulness then turned to the Marquess. "Haverton, I mean you."

It was all Lady Darlington could do to keep from going mad. She paced up and down the breakfast room, up and down the corridor, and up and down the front parlor. She thought she'd burst from the thought of Haverton and her Honoria together. He had called every day and danced with her at every party. Surely his intentions must be serious.

Voices and laughter came from the foyer. Not wanting to appear overly anxious, Lady Darlington drew in a deep, calming breath and composed herself before encountering the returning couple. The butler opened the front door allowing them to enter.

The delicious smile on Lord Haverton's lips took her breath away. He whispered to her beautiful daughter, standing by his side, and Honoria nodded and giggled. The dim-witted girl. Honoria probably had no idea what it meant to have this magnificent man hold her in such regard.

"Ah, Lady Darlington." The Marquess sketched a bow. "We have returned and I relinquish your lovely daughter to you."

Honoria giggled again.

"If I may"—he looked quite serious—"in the absence of Lord Darlington, might I have a word with you in private." His gaze momentarily darted to Honoria.

Lady Darlington was struck speechless. Could this be what she thought? Had hoped for? Was he to offer?

"Good afternoon to you, Lady Honoria, I look forward to seeing you this evening at the Lonsdale's party." Haverton turned to Lady Darlington, "I shall wait in the front parlor . . . at your convenience, madame." He followed the butler down the hall.

Lady Darlington regarded the flush over Honoria's cheeks. The color was not from too much sun or from her ride but the hue of love!

"Have you found his lordship to be agreeable?" Lady

Darlington whispered, not wishing Haverton to over-hear. It was apparent by Honoria's expression that she was quite taken by him—far more than even Lady Dar-lington had ever expected.

"Yes, Mama, I have."

"And is he with you?" As if she needed to ask . . . Haverton was ready to offer for the girl!

"Yes, Mama." A quiet, restrained excitement filled Honoria's voice.

"Oh, my dear—it is a love match!" With the much desired Marquess. "I could not be happier." Overcome by emotion she snagged the handkerchief from her sleeve and dabbed at her eyes, then at the perspiration on her flushed cheeks. Without a word, she waved Honoria away, upstairs, immediately, and the silly girl disappeared.

Lady Darlington composed herself by the time she stepped into the parlor. Haverton stood and led her to the sofa. She was much too excited to sit.

"I imagine you would not be opposed to a connection with my family?" he said in a calm that nearly caused Lady Darlington shriek.

"No, your lordship," she answered, just above a whisper. The Marquess of Haverton was what she had hoped for above all things.

"Very well. With your approval, I wish to announce your daughter's betrothal tonight at Lady Lonsdale's ball."

"Approval? Betrothal?" Lady Darlington felt the

blood drain from her head. Surely she had heard correctly. "An announcement?" She stepped forward, steadying herself at the back of the sofa. She moved to the front and settled into the seat before her knees weakened. "Object?" No, there was no objection from this quarter—not of any kind. "I could not be more pleased."

Lady Darlington could hardly contain herself. All of her plans, all of her wishes for her daughter were about to come true.

"Do you wish me to wait until your husband comes to Town to make the usual arrangements for—"

"I am sure you and Lord Darlington will manage to come to an agreement. You are quite right to go ahead with the announcement. I shall leave it up to you." Again she pressed her handkerchief to her temple.

"And would a special license be acceptable?"

"Oh, yes, a special license, if your lordship wishes. Excellent." Lady Darlington quickly agreed—the sooner the announcement and the marriage, the less time the Marquess would have to change his mind. Finally she would be connected to the Moreland family, and Honoria the Duchess to the future Duke of Waverly.

Chapter Fourteen

Haverton had the devil of a time waiting until the hour of nine that evening. His toilette, his dressing, the very time it took to travel here seemed twice as long— no, three times long, as it usually had.

He plucked at his cravat. The blessed thing wasn't standing up right and he wanted to look his best. It wasn't every day that a man announced his engagement. Haverton tugged at his cuffs that he felt were creeping up his arm into his sleeves. Would this night ever begin?

The drive to the Lonsdale residence felt excruciatingly long. Once the Marquess had arrived, he had to endure the usual greetings and salutations from the guests. He had not wished to appear rude but his thoughts were primarily on this evening's performance.

"Robert, Robert," Simon approached. Finally his brother had arrived, sounding nearly as anxious as the Marquess felt himself. "Is it time? Is it time yet?"

Simon was more of a wreck than he was. "Come, come, Simon. Honoria's not arrived yet. You do want her to be present when I announce her betrothal, don't you?"

"What?" Simon glanced around, looking for Honoria. "The angel's not arrived you say?"

"Yes, I do say." As nervous as the Marquess felt, he wasn't acting as bird-witted as his brother.

"Oh," Simon muttered, calming down a bit. "Then I say we should wait until she can join us, don't you think?"

"Yes, Simon." Haverton removed some lint from his brother's sleeve. "I think that's a splendid idea. Let's stand out of the way, over by those potted palms."

"Palms?" Simon followed Haverton to one side of the room. "Whatever for?"

"To keep you out of sight. One look at you and everyone will be able to guess something is amiss." He stepped closer and whispered, "You're all in a pucker! Come now, you must compose yourself."

Simon glanced about and gave an exasperated sigh. A few moments later he had settled down considerably.

"Good man," Haverton praised. "Now sit down"—he pushed Simon down upon a chair—"and do try to enjoy yourself." With those encouraging words he left.

If he would only stay calm, Simon would make it through the next few hours just fine. Haverton knew tonight would be perfect, a complete success. By this evening's end he, Catherine, Simon, and Honoria would be blissfully happy beyond belief. Nothing, no one, could spoil this night.

Catherine followed the Duchess into the Lonsdale's ballroom only to discover the guests who were talking with such enthusiasm and animation hushed when they entered.

"Oh, dear," Her Grace uttered softly and turned in Catherine's direction. "I believe a word of warning might be in order."

"Warning? Whatever for?" Catherine could not imagine what had made the Duchess, who was only moments ago very pleased to attend tonight's party, turn all at once grim.

"Did you not notice the room quiet as we entered? No, do not answer."

Catherine gave a slight nod.

"Can you not see how everyone observes us? No, do not look!" The Duchess opened her fan and with careful placement, held it in such a way that it hid their conversation. "It seems that we are in some way connected to the latest *on dit*." Her slow turn allowed her to scan the guests on the opposite side of the room. "If I am not mistaken, we may be rest assured that Robert is the true victim and we are targets by association."

Catherine couldn't help but glimpse at those around

her. Could the Duchess be correct? "What do you think they are saying?"

"I cannot know but I do caution you to not believe everything you may hear." The Duchess closed her fan and raised an eyebrow to Catherine in a subtle but clear warning then she strolled away. "I fear this evening is going to be a very long one."

Catherine had paced the Lonsdale's hallway twice after leaving the Duchess' company and contemplated a third length. What was she to do until the announcement? Catherine smoothed her hair in nervousness. She caught the intense tone of the conversation when nearing the end of the hallway and paused, stepping closer to catch every word.

The mention of Haverton's name caught her attention again, whereupon she once again found herself prey to Miss Price's, Miss Trueblood's, and Mrs. Baldwin's gossip mill. Catherine inched toward the trio. She ought not listen. Every instance she had done so, she had regretted the action. Another step closer still and Catherine turned her unobserved ear toward them.

"My Henrietta told me the last time he danced with her he gave her hand the most roguish squeeze just before casting off," Miss Price informed the other two women.

"Lady Joanna told me he had shamelessly flirted with her while he had partnered your Henrietta at the Stoddard's just two nights ago."

"No," Miss Price remarked in a condescending manner. "The libertine!"

"Yes," Miss Trueblood confirmed. "It's as if he hadn't a morsel of decency in him."

"He's always got his eye on the pretty ones," Miss Price countered. "I'll have that to say for him."

"Always," Miss Trueblood seconded. "I dare say he's become quite daring this Season. I wonder if he's—"

"I'm afraid none of it matters in the least," Mrs. Baldwin finally spoke, ending her silence. "He may stare, wink, and leer all he likes at your charges, it is my Honoria who has brought him up to scratch."

"Honoria?" the two chaperones cried in unison.

"Oh, yes, this very evening he is to announce their engagement."

"No," Miss Price gushed.

"Yes," Mrs. Baldwin assured her.

"No," Miss Trueblood repeated in disbelief.

"Yes," Mrs. Baldwin intoned most knowingly.

Catherine stepped away, covering her mouth, doing her best to hide her laughter.

The Duchess of Waverly stilled when she heard her son's name spoken. She stood motionless and did her best not to be noticed

"Haverton is to wed," Lady Andrew announced without preamble when she approached Mrs. Cummings-Albright in the ballroom.

"Haverton? You cannot mean—to whom?"

"It's true." Lady Andrew clasped her friend's hands, giving them a little shake. "I am so sorry but it is true, so very true."

"How do you know this?" Mrs. Cummings-Albright narrowed her eyes, scrutinizing the messenger.

"I overheard him saying as much myself at the Markham's water party just this morning. I saw them together, planning to make their announcement this very night."

"Who is she? Who is he to wed?" the Cummings-Albright woman demanded.

"Honoria Darlington."

On dit about the Darlington chit again! The Duchess knew *that* to be false. If these two ladies wished to believe that taradiddle all the better. The Cummings-Albright woman could well cause problems.

"I won't allow it!" she cried, trying to keep her voice low, and pushed at Lady Andrew who grasped her arms to keep them still.

The Duchess had never cared for Mrs. Cummings-Albright and was quite relieved when she and Robert parted company at the end of last Season.

"Celeste, my dear," Lady Andrew pleaded, trying to calm her, "people will hear you—remember where you are."

"He can't marry her! He is mine, do you understand? Mine!"

"Please, restrain yourself," Lady Andrew implored, reaching out her hand to cease the outburst. "If he's already made up his mind, I'm not so sure what you can do about it."

"I'll stop him! I won't let him get away with this." She appeared to the Duchess to be very desperate or on the edge of madness. "I'll think of a way to—"

"Look there, Celeste." Lady Andrew pointed to the entrance with the tip of her closed fan. The two women watched Robert and Simon enter the ballroom.

"Take note of Lord Simon," Mrs. Cummings-Albright replied with a tone altogether different from her ranting of moments ago. "See how unsettled he appears."

Simon appeared very agitated. The Duchess wished he had a portion of his elder brother's ability to display a granite facade. Apparently he had none of that talent. Not more than a minute later, Lady Darlington and Honoria entered. Haverton's smile appeared to be more paternal than swainlike.

"Do you notice how Haverton shows so little interest in Honoria Darlington?" Mrs. Cummings-Albright pointed out to Lady Andrew. "*If* he is to marry the Darlington chit . . . unless . . . unless he is not to marry her after all."

"Perhaps he is only pretending disinterest to avoid suspicion," Lady Andrew suggested.

"I do not know." Mrs. Cummings-Albright began to scan the room. "But I am going to find out. And then I will stop them."

The Duchess realized that Haverton must act quickly.

The sooner Robert's and Catherine's announcement was made the better.

Mrs. Cummings-Albright watched Haverton from the other side of the ballroom. There was no mistaking the pure delight shining in his eyes as he took uninhibited pleasure in laying eyes upon Miss Hayward, and Mrs. Cummings-Albright would have to be blind not to notice.

"Look how Haverton stares but not at Lady Honoria. And see how she looks in his direction, however not at the Marquess. It seems to me that it is Lord Simon who returns her adoration. I believe Lord Haverton's attention is quite fixed on his mother's ward Miss Hayward."

The Duchess sighed. *This could well be a problem.*

It was very strange how neither Catherine nor Honoria were dancing. At every other party they'd attended, both were engaged for every dance. There was certainly something peculiar in the atmosphere tonight.

"What are you doing?" Honoria Darlington asked Catherine with a quizzical expression. "Are you eavesdropping?"

Catherine jumped. "Oh!" She wouldn't have admitted it but she'd been caught. "I am so ashamed. I simply could not help herself."

"Well?" Honoria moved closer. "Who were you listening to? What were they saying?"

It seemed Lady Honoria had the same bad habit of

eavesdropping as Catherine. "I'm afraid I heard your chaperone giving her contemporaries an update."

Honoria peered around Catherine, observing the gossiping trio in action. Their furtive head gestures and weighted glances had continued when Catherine had long stopped listening.

"Those old women are no better than they should be." Honoria bristled, turning the other way in disapproval.

"But they are such fun," Catherine enlightened her. "Mrs. Baldwin is so proud that you've managed to catch Lord Haverton's fancy. I've heard her say you are betrothed and he is to make the announcement this very night." She widened her eyes in astonishment.

A small crease appeared on Honoria's forehead. "I do hope she won't be too disappointed when it comes out that it's not exactly true."

Catherine leaned forward and whispered, holding back her laughter. "I think they'll be too shocked to be disappointed."

"They all will be so surprised. Look, there is Simon—" Honoria grasped Catherine's arm and led her toward the potted palms in the corner. "You must come with me."

"What?"

Honoria brought Catherine along before she could utter a single word of protest. "I cannot stand here alone, for it would look quite odd, do you not think?"

"But why on Earth should we stand here?" Catherine thought it odd.

"Simon is seated just on the other side of this palm."

Catherine could see the potted palm but did not see a single sign of Lord Simon.

"No, don't look!" Honoria scolded.

"I'm sorry." Catherine pulled back, returning to her side of the potted plant.

"Just stand there and pretend we are having a conversation," Honoria instructed, trying her best to ignore the palm.

Catherine kept careful watch and tried not to appear out of the ordinary, while having her imaginary conversation with Honoria.

"Simon?" Honoria whispered between the palm fronds. "Simon? Can you hear me?"

"Is that you, my pet?" a man's voice returned.

"Goose!" Honoria giggled. "I don't think I can manage another moment without seeing you." She reached around the palm, grasping for his hand.

"Honoria, please! Someone will see you," Catherine warned.

"Just a moment more," she begged. "When is Lord Haverton going to get on with it?"

"Soon, dearest, soon," Simon swore. "I think I shall urge him to do so this minute."

"Yes, yes. I don't want to wait a moment longer." After Simon had gone off, Honoria pressed her hand to her cheek. She glanced up expectantly at Catherine. "I'm going to find Mama. Will you come with me, Catherine?"

"I think if Lord Haverton's going to make his announcement, I'd best find the Duchess."

"Very well, I expect we all shall have a grand celebration afterwards!" Honoria smiled at Catherine and took her leave.

Chapter Fifteen

Haverton had walked up and down the gallery several times since he'd left his brother seated near the palms. He had just returned to the ballroom when Simon rushed up to him with set deliberation.

"Come now, I must insist that you delay no longer. Please, Robert, Honoria and I—will you end this waiting?" He sounded quite desperate. "What do you say?"

Haverton laughed. A nervous laugh. Simon was right. It was time. Before beginning, he needed to assemble all parties involved. "Why don't you find Mother and Catherine and I'll gather Honoria and her mother. We'll meet in the library and all go out together."

"Yes, yes, a capital idea. Capital!" Simon rushed off to do his part.

Some minutes later, the Marquess had found Honoria

and Lady Darlington and led them into the library where Lady Lonsdale waited. She had already been informed by the Duchess that her family wished to make an announcement. From what Haverton could see, the hostess was more than delighted to have this event—whatever it was to be since she did not know—occur at her party. Apparently she had heard from some of the guests that he would break the news of his impending nuptials at her soiree tonight!

"Honoria, it is time. It is nearly time!" Lady Darlington trembled with excitement.

"Please calm yourself, Mama," Honoria urged with her face flushed. She didn't appear much calmer than her mother. "You'll swoon before Haverton has a chance to speak and miss the whole thing."

"No, I shan't do that. I wouldn't miss this for the world!"

"Where is the Duchess?" Lady Lonsdale peered about as excited as any of the rest of them.

"Please wait here," the Marquess instructed. "Simon is looking for her. I'll see what's keeping them." Leaving the three ladies, Haverton marched off toward the ballroom.

Catherine had spotted Haverton in the corridor just outside the ballroom and tried not to meet his gaze. If she had there was no doubt that everyone would know how she felt about him. Everyone. And she didn't want to ruin their plan, especially when they were so close to putting an end to the charade.

She stood in the doorway, wringing her hands. Catherine had not found the Duchess in the refreshment room and decided to return to the ballroom where she must have overlooked Her Grace. Before Catherine could leave, a footman handed her a note. She stepped aside to read the missive in private.

His lordship asks that you meet him concerning a matter most urgent. Please wait for him abovestairs, in the west wing, down the second corridor, last room on the left. Honoria

Catherine dreaded to think what might have happened. Were their evening's plans called off? Surely it was something so dreadful that Haverton could not write himself. Catherine clutched the note and headed for the staircase, keeping careful watch that she wasn't followed.

Up the stairs she climbed to the first floor. Catherine gazed down the darkened west wing before deciding she needed to first venture into the east wing for a source of illumination. Within five minutes she was moving down the seemingly deserted part of the house. Down, down to the end of the corridor. She could see the dead end. Catherine turned toward the last door on the left and glanced around before letting herself in.

"Haverton?" she called out tentatively. Catherine walked into the room and held her candle high, peering into the darkness. A floorboard groaned and perhaps there was the squeak from a rusty door hinge. "Is that you, my lord?"

She moved to the left side of the room, near an opened door, and stepped closer to see what lay beyond. Catherine peered past a doorway. A sharp shove between her shoulder blades pushed her to the ground into what she then realized was a closet. The door slammed shut and the scrape of something heavy moving over the floor came to a rest before it.

"No!" she cried in the darkness. Catherine had dropped her candle when she fell, the flame snuffed out soon after. Pushing to her knees, she moved to the door and pounded with both fists. "Let me out—please!"

Listening intently, Catherine heard the creak of a door hinge followed by utter silence which told her the attacker had fled. She was alone in the most remote area in an unused wing of a grand London mansion. Here in the small, darkened room, she imagined that she might never be found—not found alive, anyway.

The closet was dusty, the air stuffy. She sat, resting her back against the door, blinking into the darkness. If she heard a sound, any sound, Catherine would pound on the door and scream until she could cry out no longer but for now there was only silence.

Neither the darkness nor the small room especially

frightened her. Catherine could only sit and wait. Isolated and alone, it might be possible that no one would ever find her. If she were to die here, the one regret she would truly have would be that she never told Haverton how much she cared, how much she loved him. Her Robert.

At least no one was there to see her cry.

In the ballroom Lady Lonsdale interrupted the party and gave Haverton the floor.

"I'm sorry for disrupting your evening, ladies and gentlemen, but I have an announcement." During this momentary pause, Haverton noticed Celeste hovering about the door, the far door. He resumed his speech, "I am very pleased to announce the engagement of Lady Honoria Darlington"—a flood of whispers swept through the room in speculation—"to my brother Lord Simon Moreland."

Shrieks and gasps of surprise echoed through the room.

"Did you hear? Haverton remains eligible!" came a solitary female voice from the crowd.

Lady Darlington promptly swooned, nearly hitting the floor.

"Mama!" Honoria cried out.

Simon dashed to his future mother-in-law's side in a trice and caught her before she had landed on the floor in a heap.

"My word," said Lady Lonsdale.

"There is still a chance for you, my dear!" came another, sounding relieved.

Another woman cried out, "All is not yet lost!"

"This has come as a shock to more than a few of you I see," the Marquess remarked.

The Duchess made sure their hostess was well out of hearing range before asking Haverton, "What of you and Catherine? Where is she?" She glanced about the room.

"She is nowhere to be found." His voice cracked with emotion. He glanced toward the door where he'd seen Celeste earlier and an uneasy feeling came over him. "This is all so terribly wrong." The Marquess rubbed his eyes and swallowed hard. "This was not the way we planned. I cannot imagine her absence is accidental. Do not worry, Mother. I will find her."

Haverton now stood in the foyer and stared down the long corridor toward the ballroom. He looked from side to side, allowing himself to imagine the rooms that lay beyond and the hallways that led in those directions.

He travelled through the hallway of the main floor checking the library, breakfast room, and several parlors both small and large. Haverton was certain she was not on this floor. He was equally as sure she had not gone off on her own accord. Returning to the place where he'd begun his search, his stared upward to the next floor, accessed by the grand staircase.

It then crossed his mind how many times he'd been

an unwilling visitor in an out-of-the-way closet—he was ashamed to admit it but the incident occurred more than one would imagine.

If it had worked for him, why not Catherine?

The Marquess ascended the stairs to the first-floor landing. He strode down the obviously lived-in east wing, calling out her name. There was no answer. Then he headed down the darkened west wing. He went in search of some light.

The corridor seemed as if it went on forever. He called out her name as he passed. The corridor came to a dead end. He pushed open the door on the right, stepped inside, and lifted the candelabrum to illuminate the room. Nothing.

Haverton stepped back into the hallway and entered the room on the left. "Catherine!" Had he heard something—a scrape? A sob?

"Robert!" came the muffled cry.

The Marquess strode into the room and saw a chest blocking a door. Stepping closer, the illumination showed tracks on the floor that told him the chest had been moved recently. "Catherine, are you all right?"

"Yes. Oh, yes!" He heard her sob. "It's dark and—"

"Give me a moment, I'll have you out in a thrice." He set the candelabrum on a covered table to the side before pushing the chest back. Haverton pulled open the door and Catherine ran into his arms. He held her tight. "It's all right. I've got you. You're fine now."

"I was so frightened." Her tears subsided. "I didn't

think anyone would ever find me. I was trapped . . . I—"

"Who's done this to you?" Haverton pulled her from him. He had to see for himself that she was unharmed.

"I don't know. I never saw their face." She began to swipe at her skirts, brushing away the dust.

"It does not matter. You are safe with me, and I shall not allow you out of my sight." He brought her hand to his lip and kissed it. "What's that you've got here?"

Crumpled in her hand was a small parchment. "It's the note from Honoria telling me to meet you here."

He glanced at her. "I sent no such note."

"I know that now."

The Marquess smoothed the paper to read it. They were not his words, and if he was not mistaken, this was not written in Honoria's hand. He recognized the writing to be Celeste Cummings-Albright's.

"Come with me," he said, reaching for the branch of candles. "I believe I've had enough of these wicked schemes and countless untruths. Something must be done, we can no longer allow anyone to—"

"Robert, I–I'm afraid." Her voice grew quiet. "I don't want to face those people."

"You won't be doing it alone. We must," he told her. "We must show them all that we will do as we wish, despite what they've all heard, and we are not to be manipulated by their malicious gossip. Threatening to make us social outcasts—I could not care less if any of those people ever acknowledged me again." His voice softened. "Yours is the only opinion that matters."

She smiled. "And I must tell you that I, as are many of the ladies in Town, am completely enamored of you. You have won my heart and I can deny you nothing." The fear from her frightening ordeal and the strain she had imagined in facing those who might have caused this unpleasantness evaporated. "I will stand by your side, my lord."

"You are not simply *another* lady in Town." He stepped near and held her close. "You have a very great power over me and it is more than the threat that you may gossip about my fondness for plying watercolors and make me a social outcast."

"I would never—" She gasped, mocking outrage. "Your secret is safe with me."

"Just as I suspected." He bent and kissed her cheek before leading her to the door.

"Besides, if I were to let it be known that the Marquess of Haverton's hobby is watercolor landscapes, there'll be a run on art supplies. The gentlemen's clubs will empty and their patrons will cover the parks, riverbanks, and every scenic spot around Town with their easels."

Catherine fairly ran after the Marquess as he strode down the west corridor with her hand in his. He must have felt that she encumbered his progress for he set the candelabrum on a table, swept her into his arms, and proceeded down the staircase. Reaching the ground floor, he continued toward the guests.

Near the entrance, Catherine observed the familiar gathering of heads as groups of people came together in conversation. The rapid succession of people regrouping to those around them told Catherine word was spreading fast.

The Marquess of Haverton strode into the ballroom with Catherine in his arms. She caught sight of the Duchess of Waverly as they passed. The Duchess brought her hand to her throat and her eyes widened with apparent shock. Lord Simon wrapped his arm around Lady Honoria's shoulder and drew her near. Lady Darlington clutched his arm on his opposite side for support. Apparently that arrangement had worked out well.

Haverton paused in front of Mrs. Cummings-Albright and grumbled an angry, "Do not think your actions will be overlooked. Count yourself lucky. If any harm should have come to Miss Hayward I would have made certain the consequences would have been most harsh."

Slowly at first, the guests drew away from Mrs. Cummings-Albright until she stood alone and quite isolated. She glanced at those around her, noting her prompt rejection from polite society, and raised her gloved hand to cover her sobs before fleeing from the room.

The guests around them parted, their curiosity palpable. When the Marquess reached the center of the room he set Catherine upon her feet.

"My lords and ladies, gentlemen and gentlewomen. I beg your indulgence as I make my true confession before you and deny the gossipmongers throughout Town the opportunity to distort the facts. I stand before you, in plain sight, so there will be no doubt as to my actions or motives."

A multitude of gasps echoed throughout the room in the stunned silence.

Haverton turned toward Catherine. "I beg your forgiveness, my sweet, for making what should be a most private and intimate moment a public display." He lowered himself, bending on one knee before her.

More muffled cries of shock came from around the room. Haverton could feel the piercing stares of everyone in attendance and by Catherine's reaction, she had felt them too. She could not seem to pull her gaze away from the crowd of people who stared at her. She felt more terrified than when Haverton had found her barricaded in the closet.

"Miss Hayward." He drew her attention away from the surrounding crowd. "My dear Miss Hayward." He gained and held her complete attention so she would close out the others. "Catherine, I must confess my genuine affection for you and beg you to become my wife."

"No!" one woman cried out. There were many high-pitched cries that echoed across the room and several loud sobs followed.

"It is my unfortunate role in life but I must ask you to

bear the burden of my title which would make you the marchioness of Haverton and, sometime in the future, the Duchess of Waverly."

Out came the melodic alto and tenor wails of mothers who had their hearts set on the Marquess as a son-in-law, whose hopes were finally and irrevocably dashed.

"This cannot be!" came another shout of outrage.

"For these past few years I have been plagued by various women who have been relentless in their pursuit and I am remiss if I am not completely honest with you and say that it may not end even though I am wed. However I vow, before all these people as my witness, my love and my fidelity."

Sobs punctuated the pauses all through his discourse. The soaring soprano's vibrating note sounded almost like an aria in the background of Haverton's pronouncement.

"I ask you to become my wife because I cannot tolerate another day without your presence in my life. I need to see your smile, your face. I need to hear your sweet voice. Your laughter brings me more joy than even I can imagine."

"All is lost!" came the plaintiff wail. "Say it is not so!"

More soft weeping whispered around him. The younger women, he guessed. Something he'd said must have struck a chord.

"I love you and the notion of continuing without you . . . life would have no meaning."

Multiple cries of "No!" rang out around them, followed by wholehearted sobs that echoed around the room. The crying went on and on.

"I have procured a special license so we may wed as soon as possible." The Marquess continued to look up into her eyes and asked his final question. "What say you, Miss Hayward? Will you do me the honor of marrying me?"

Catherine remained quiet.

"Of course she's going to say yes," some woman called out quite spitefully among the waterworks around the room.

The surrounding guests blowing their noses in quite unladylike fashion made a horrendous racket more akin to a flock of geese than gentle-bred females. Several high-pitched tantrums played out, much to the dismay of the mothers or the young ladies' companions who tried to keep their wards silent.

Catherine glanced at Haverton and replied, "Yes, my lord." Her answer was nearly inaudible but he saw her lips move, forming the words. She said louder, nearly shouting. "I accept."

"You see there, ladies? I am a most fortunate man. She'll have me!" He stood, smiling, waving his arm in victory. "You have made me happy beyond belief." He kissed her gloved hand before setting it in the crook of his arm and led her toward the door.

The Duchess stood by her youngest son Simon and his Honoria. Her Grace watched her eldest and his fiancée pass her to quit the ballroom. Catherine and Robert would soon be married and he would provide the long-awaited heir. Until that moment, the Duchess never knew how much she longed to be a grandmother.

The wailing of the females, young and old, did not cease.

"You should all be ashamed of yourselves!" Her Grace reprimanded.

An embarrassed hush fell over the crowd.

She then remarked, "Is no one happy when true love takes its course?"

F Marks
Marks, Shirley.

His lordship's chaperone